"I thought I was in love with you then."

Lauren's lips curved in a disdainful smile. "But fortunately I grew out of such childish fancies."

"Did you?" Joe's dark eyes held hers in the soft glow of the nightclub's subtle lighting. "So if I asked you now to marry me...?"

Not by a quaver did Lauren reveal how much his words had startled her. "Marry you?" she responded as contemptuously as she dared. "After all these years? How very romantic! But I don't think so."

A shadow of hot anger passed behind his eyes. "Be careful Lauren," he warned, his voice menacingly soft. "You're making me bid very high for what I want." His dark eyes swept possessively over her body.

A cold chill of fear fluttered around Lauren's heart, knowing well that when Joe Daley wanted something, he got it.

SUSANNE McCARTHY has spent most of her life in London, but after her marriage she and her husband moved to Shropshire, and the author is now an enthusiastic advocate of this unspoiled part of England. So although her first romance novel, *A Long Way from Heaven*, was set in the sunny Caribbean, Susanne says that the English countryside may feature in her future writing.

SUSANNE McCARTHY

a long way from heaven

Harlequin Books

TORONTO • NEW YORK • LONDON
AMSTERDAM • PARIS • SYDNEY • HAMBURG
STOCKHOLM • ATHENS • TOKYO • MILAN

Harlequin Presents first edition May 1987
ISBN 0-373-10979-2

Original hardcover edition published in 1986
by Mills & Boon Limited

CHAPTER ONE

'WELL, well, if it isn't the merry widow!'

Lauren turned slowly at the sound of that familiar voice. In ten years in the Caribbean islands, Joe Daley had not lost his New York drawl. 'Why, Joe,' she responded with a cool smile, 'how kind of you to come over so promptly to pay your condolences!'

'How could I resist the opportunity to see you in black, sweetheart? It always was your colour.'

His eyes swept down over her in unhurried appraisal. She was indeed wearing black, but the dress could hardly be described as mourning. It was a clinging sheath of silk jersey, cut low over the honey-smooth curve of her breasts, the svelte skirt moulding her long slender legs seductively.

'The show must go on,' she returned, unruffled. 'I have a nightclub to run.'

'How brave,' he drawled, a mocking laugh in his voice. 'You hide your heartbreak well.'

Lauren's dark eyes flashed. Though she was too honest to pretend a grief she did not feel, Joe's cynicism infuriated her. She turned him an aloof shoulder as Raoul, her head croupier, approached discreetly to consult her on the amount of credit to be extended to a certain customer.

'He's already down six and a half thousand dollars,' Raoul whispered, leaning close to her ear, 'but he's been into us for twice that and paid up.'

'Very well, let it go for now. But if he gets close to ten thousand, come and tell me.'

'Yes, ma'am.'

Raoul withdrew, and Lauren turned back to her unwelcome guest. 'You'll have a drink with me?' she invited in a voice that hinted that the politeness was the merest formality.

'I'd be delighted,' he responded, his smile indicating that he found her reluctance amusing.

She laid her slender hand on his arm, and allowed him to lead her from the dark green smoky cavern of the gaming room into the softly-lit nightclub. A stool at the end of the bar, close to the curtained archway that separated the two rooms, was always reserved for her. From here she could survey the whole room, and into the supper room beyond. She rested one elbow lightly on the bar, crossing her long legs elegantly.

The barman materialised as if on cue as they sat down. 'Bring up a bottle of the Bollinger '79, Harry,' said Joe.

'Sure, boss. Hey, boss, that right you caught a Great White off Prickly Point, weighed more than five thousand pounds?'

Joe laughed. 'I didn't catch it, Harry. One of my guests caught it off the *Midnight Lady*.'

'Yeah, but you was steering the boat, wasn't you, boss?' Harry persisted. Joe conceded a nod, and Harry went away, muttering to himself in satisfaction, 'Ain't the man that holds the line that catches the fish. Big old shark like that, you gotta get the boat just right . . .'

Lauren laughed without humour. 'I see my staff still hero-worship you, Joe,' she remarked dryly. 'No wonder you like coming over here!'

'Ah, the Blue Lagoon has many attractions,' he returned suavely, and the way he allowed his eyes to linger over the slender curves of her body left her in no doubt that he counted her as one of the prime attractions.

'I do wish you wouldn't encourage them to go on calling you boss,' she snapped a little sharply. 'It's seven years since you were boss around here.'

'Maybe they think it won't be long before I'm boss here again,' he suggested, his smile taunting her.

'I doubt it,' she responded with asperity.

His reply was that maddeningly enigmatic smile.

Harry returned with the champagne, and opened it with a flourish, spilling the sparkling foam into a pair of tulip glasses. Lauren savoured the bouquet, one finely-drawn eyebrow lifted in cool enquiry. 'Do you really think this is in quite the best of taste, Joe, considering the circumstances?'

'Surely Blanc-de-Noirs is never in bad taste?' he countered.

'You don't feel it might give the impression that we're celebrating?' she queried dryly.

'But of course. Surely that's exactly what we are doing?'

His dark eyes were always difficult for her to fathom, but tonight he was being particularly enigmatic. Anyone watching them would have thought them the perfect pair. He so tall, the well-cut formality of his white dinner-jacket emphasising rather than concealing his powerful build. He would have been a match for any of Lauren's tough nightclub bouncers— and that, she knew, was how he had started his career. He was a mongrel from Brooklyn. The black hair suggested a dash of Italian blood, and the air of cool self-possession came from growing up hard on the streets.

But there was intelligence as well as ruthlessness in the handsome rawboned face. He had been Lauren's

father's right-hand man for three years when he first
came to the Grenadines, running the Blue Lagoon
with a skill that had drawn from it a profit it had not
made before or since.

He owned his own place now, over at Hurricane Bay
on the island's rugged Atlantic coast. It was one of the
top night-spots in the West Indies, attracting high-
rollers from all over the world to its luxurious
facilities. How Joe had managed to buy it, only four
years after leaving her father's employment, had been
the subject of much speculation.

When he had first returned to Hurricane Bay, it
was said that his relationship with Magda Coburn,
the owner, was a good deal more intimate than
either of them would admit. Lauren had found that
hard to believe. Joe was far too proud a man to
stoop to being what was little better than a gigolo.
When Magda left the island to return to the States,
it had seemed that she had left Joe to manage her
property. But it soon became apparent that he was,
in fact, the owner.

Gossip had been rife. The story most widely
accredited was that he had won Hurricane Bay from
Magda's late husband in a card game, and it was even
speculated that Karl might have taken his own life as a
result, though the official version was that he had died
of a heart attack. Then Joe was said to be hand-in-
glove with the racketeers who still used the islands as a
staging post for their illegal activities. Lauren had seen
for herself the mysterious man from New York who
sometimes stayed at Hurricane Bay as Joe's personal
guest. Joe called him Rick; no one knew his other
name. He was always surrounded by a vicious-looking
entourage, but though he himself was neither tall nor
well-built, there was an air of personal menace about

him that was so chilling that no one ever looked him in the eye.

Hurricane Bay had prospered under Joe's control, unscrupulously poaching the best customers and the best staff from its rivals. And the strongest rival to Joe's casino had always been the Blue Lagoon, where he now sat sipping the crisp champagne, his dark eyes studying the woman who had been the daughter, then the wife, and was now owner in her own right. Her sleek, raven-black hair was swept into an elegant chignon that emphasised the sensitive length of her neck. Her face was fine-boned and aristocratic, giving the clue to the hidalgo Spanish blood that flowed in her veins. Her skin glowed creamy-gold, smooth as silk over her slender shoulders and down to the temptingly soft curve of her breasts.

She was tall for a woman—the high heels of her evening sandals took her to a willowy six feet. She had an air of delicacy that Joe knew was deceptive. Once he could have read every thought in those liquid dark eyes. But the years that had matured the coltish teenager into a lovely young woman of twenty-five had changed her in more subtle ways. She had an air of mystery that intrigued him.

Her voice was low and husky—but then it always was—as she asked, 'What exactly are we supposed to be celebrating, Joe?'

He cast his eyes round the nightclub, crowded with the smart and sophisticated élite who could afford to cruise their luxury yachts around the resort night-spots of the West Indies. 'Your inheritance?' he suggested.

Her glance followed his. The Blue Lagoon was certainly a worthy rival to Hurricane Bay. A series of arches leading from one area to another, white walls contrasting starkly with a floor of gleaming dark African mahogany, heavy bronze satin curtains and lots of rich leather upholstery underlined the cool Spanish atmosphere that was very popular with the rich visitors to the island.

Lauren's silky lashes veiled her eyes as she studied her companion. She smiled slowly, and raised her glass to her lips. 'Ah yes, my inheritance,' she purred. 'That's worth a toast.'

'What will you do with it now?' asked Joe with apparently casual interest.

'Do?' she repeated, pretending not to know what he meant.

'Yes. Surely you won't try to continue running the casino on your own?'

'But of course I will, Joe,' she smiled sweetly. 'Why shouldn't I?'

'You enjoy presiding over gaming tables?' he asked harshly.

I hate it! But aloud she said, 'Certainly. It's very lucrative. But you know that, don't you? Hurricane Bay must have made you a fortune. I daresay you're a millionaire by now.'

'I daresay,' he conceded dryly. 'But running a casino is hardly a job for a woman.'

'I've run it for seven years on my own. I got little help from my father or my husband. Now it's mine, without claim or hindrance from anyone else,' Lauren asserted, mentally setting aside the stack of mortgages that faced her. Her eyes met his levelly. 'I don't intend to let it go,' she added with quiet determination.

The Blue Lagoon was her home, the only home she had ever known. She had stayed here through seven years of a bitterly unhappy marriage, and she wasn't going to leave it now; not for Joe Daley, not for anyone.

Joe was watching her, a taunting smile playing round his hard, level mouth. 'Then perhaps we should drink to your freedom?' he went on provocatively.

Lauren flashed him a look of such icy contempt as would have quelled any other man on the spot, but Joe merely returned her a look of quizzical amusement.

'Why the frosty glare?' he enquired sardonically. 'Don't try to tell me you were in love with Bill Henderson!'

'Shouldn't I have been?' she returned with dignity. 'I was married to him for seven years.'

'That doesn't mean you married him for love,' he pointed out cynically.

'Ah, the voice of an expert on the subject,' she retorted, unable to keep the cutting edge from her voice. He acknowledged her slip with a knowing smile. 'You're implying that I married him for money?' she defended swiftly. 'You *do* credit me with a mercenary heart! I was only seventeen.'

His smile held a hint of reminiscence. 'So you were,' he murmured. 'And a beauty even then. Henderson could never complain that he didn't get good value for his money.' Her eyes kindled, angrily meeting his mocking amusement. 'Oh, I'm not saying it was your idea,' he added sardonically. 'You did have a certain innocence in those days. I don't doubt it was your father who first thought of it.'

'I see you have it all worked out,' remarked Lauren tightly.

He leaned towards her, his voice low and compelling. 'Come on, Lauren. I was the manager here, remember? I know how much trouble he was in. He as good as sold you to the highest bidder.'

'How dare you say that?' she snarled furiously.

'You know it's the truth,' he insisted, his dark perceptive eyes watching for any sign of weakness.

She leashed her temper with difficulty. Joe was deliberately goading her, and she would not give him the satisfaction of letting slip the mask of cool self-possession behind which she had hidden for so long. 'Nevertheless, I needed little persuasion,' she reminded him, a satisfied little smile curving her delicate lips.

'No, you didn't, did you?' he returned sneeringly. 'I hope it was worth it.'

'Oh, it was,' she purred, sipping her champagne. 'I found that I have very expensive tastes.'

One dark eyebrow lifted fractionally. 'Strange,' he drawled in that smokily seductive voice that could usually melt any woman's resistance. 'I remember that once you were ready to run away to New York with a penniless mongrel.'

Lauren felt a soft tinge of pink steal across her cheeks. Joe had touched a raw nerve. Seven years ago she had adored Joe Daley with all the innocence and vulnerability of her seventeen years, and he had betrayed her. She had been too young to take that kind of pain. She had been devastated by it, not caring what happened to her. And in that state she had let her father talk her into marrying Bill Henderson. She had paid bitterly for that mistake. The first few months of her marriage had been a nightmare from which there had been no waking.

But her pride had always held her back from letting anyone know the secrets in her heart. Her lips curved in a disdainful smile. 'Oh yes, I thought I was in love with you then,' she admitted, her eyes glittering as dangerously as black ice, 'but fortunately I grew out of such childish fancies.'

'Did you?' Two pairs of dark eyes met and held in the soft glow of the nightclub's subtle lighting. Two masters of the game of poker sought to guess the thoughts that each concealed so well. 'So if I asked you now to marry me . . .?'

Not by a quaver did Lauren reveal how much his words had startled her. 'Marry you, Joe?' she responded as disdainfully as she dared. 'After all these years? How very romantic! But I don't think so.'

A shadow of hot anger passed behind his eyes. 'Be careful, Lauren,' he warned, his voice menacingly soft. 'You're making me bid very high for what I want, and I don't intend to lose.' A cold chill of fear fluttered round Lauren's heart, but she met his searing gaze defiantly. 'I'll own this place, and I'll own you.' His dark eyes swept possessively over her body, making her flesh burn as if he had touched her. 'I've waited a long time.'

Abruptly he sat back, changing the mood with bewildering suddenness. He raised his glass to her in sardonic salute. 'So I give you our toast,' he said, at his most urbane. 'To memories.'

When he chose, his smile could be quite devastatingly attractive. But Lauren had burned in his flame a long time ago, and now she was fireproof. She held his gaze unwaveringly, and chinked her glass against his. 'To memories,' she repeated softly.

Joe sipped his champagne, and with calculated insolence allowed his gaze to rove around the room, seeking out the prettiest girls. He chose a petite blonde, singling her out with one lingering look from those mesmerising dark eyes. The girl blushed, and looked away, but inevitably her eyes returned to flirt with his.

'Not that one, Joe,' Lauren murmured dryly.

He slanted her a speculative gaze. 'Jealous, sweetheart?'

'Not at all,' she responded, matching his sardonic tone, 'but she's one of Sheik Jabul's harem. You wouldn't want to precipitate another oil crisis, would you?'

He twirled his glass thoughtfully. 'Why not?' he mused, deliberately provocative. 'It might be rather entertaining.'

'Are you so very bored?' she enquired without sympathy.

He shrugged his wide shoulders in cool indifference. 'The palate becomes a trifle jaded,' he drawled laconically. 'Women are all pretty much the same, when you get right down to it. After a while a little extra spice is needed to liven things up.'

Lauren fought to leash her temper. 'Indeed?' she queried tautly. 'Then since you find us all so dull, I'll relieve you of my company. Please excuse me.' As she stepped through the curtain into the gaming room she heard his mocking laughter behind her.

'How are we doing, Raoul?' she asked quietly.

'Not badly, Mrs Henderson,' he answered in a low tone. 'I'm afraid Mr Georgiou is down another thousand.' His eyes slid expressively towards the roulette table. 'He's trying the Biarritz system tonight.' He allowed the faintest glimmer of a smile to steal across his well-schooled countenance. 'Someone should tell him that no system can ever beat the table,' he added dryly.

Mr Georgiou was at his usual seat, his gold pen flying over his notepad as he calculated and recalculated the odds. He was betting heavily on the number eight, and biting his lip with anxiety.

The croupier, Lascelles, spun the wheel, calling in a hushed voice, '*Rien ne va plus. Ne va plus, maintenant.*' Lauren moved a little closer. '*Vingt-stept,*' announced Lascelles clearly. 'Twenty-seven.'

'Bad luck, Mr Georgiou,' consoled Lauren with professional sympathy.

His eyes flew up to her face. 'Ah, Mrs Henderson! You look charming tonight, charming. Stay. Maybe you'll bring me luck.'

She laughed lightly. 'But if I do that, Mr Georgiou, it would be I who would be losing,' she reminded him gently.

'*Faites vos jeux, mesdames, messieurs,*' chanted Lascelles in his softly-accented Creole French. Like Raoul and most of the other croupiers at the Blue Lagoon, he was from Martinique, and was justifiably proud of his style and skill.

Lauren moved on, casting her eyes over the blackjack tables. The one-dollar table had closed at midnight—it was merely a concession to the light-hearted. The serious gamblers would sit around the five-dollar tables until the casino closed at dawn. She glanced towards the baccarat table; a hushed intensity about the players told her that the stakes were running high. That was good; the bank should always have the edge, and that edge was the casino's profit. Yes, it promised to be a good night—and how badly she needed nights like this!

When she returned to the bar, Joe had gone. Musingly she poured herself another glass of champagne. They had drunk to memories—memories of that long-ago summer when this champagne had been laid down in the cool stone cellars beneath her feet. It was as near perfect now as champagne could be; beautifully balanced, with a hint of wood-age to broaden out the flavour, but not so much as to overpower its delicacy. If it had been tasted prematurely, seven years ago, it would have been young and green, lacking the subtlety that seduced the palate.

She gazed into the sparkling heart of the glass. Seven years ago she too had been young and green, a naïve little fool, seventeen years old and wearing her heart on her sleeve. She had believed that Joe had loved her, and her trusting innocence had made her an easy victim for his ruthless charm. But the years had taught her some hard lessons, and she no longer had any romantic illusions. Love was no part of Joe Daley's repertoire.

And yet he had offered her marriage. He certainly was bidding high. Since his return to the island of St Arnoux he had taken to visiting his nearest rival about once a month, sometimes alone, sometimes with a party of his big-spending friends. On those occasions, her husband had played least-in-sight. It was commonly accepted that he was afraid of Joe.

Joe had never troubled to disguise his admiration of the beautiful Mrs Henderson. Several times, when he was between mistresses, he had hinted that if she cared to leave her husband, she could seek his 'protection'. She had always accepted his slightly mocking homage with insouciance, and over the years their relationship had settled into a sort of armed truce.

Lauren knew that many people believed that they were secretly lovers. While her husband was alive the situation had had a certain piquancy that had intrigued the gossip-loving jet-setters who patronised the two casinos. But now she no longer had the shield of her phoney marriage to hide behind. If she continued to resist Joe's advances he would be made to look a fool. And Joe Daley would never allow that to happen.

Her eyes roved again around the crowded nightclub. She was aware that her conversation with Joe had been watched with avid interest by many eyes. No one would be surprised that Joe would want to marry her. The Blue Lagoon was a very attractive proposition. It was one of the finest luxury resorts in the Caribbean islands.

St Arnoux was one of the smaller islands of the Windward chain, set among the Grenadines south of St Vincent. Barely two miles from north to south, it was mostly covered by the densely-wooded slopes of the extinct volcano that rose to nearly three hundred feet at its centre. The few hundred inhabitants lived in the settlement—it could barely be called a village—that clustered in the shelter of a ruined fort at the northernmost tip of the island, making their living from the myriad fish that could be caught in the sapphire waters or from catering to the wishes of the millionaire pleasure-seekers who flocked to its sparkling shores in their luxury yachts and schooners.

The Blue Lagoon ought to be making a handsome profit. Set in a hollow of the hill on the island's tranquil south-western shore, the palm-fringed beach of shining white sand ran down to a wide lagoon, sheltered by a coral reef, that offered perfect facilities for many water sports. Most of the guests stayed on their yachts, moored at the long wooden jetty, but some chose to rent one of the bungalows dotted in peaceful seclusion among the waving casuarinas.

The main building, which housed every facility that the wealthy patrons could want, was an elegant mansion built in Spanish Hacienda style. It lay back where the ground began to rise to the slopes of the

volcano beyond. French windows led from the supper
room and nightclub on to a wide terrace, so that
during the warm evenings outdoors and indoors
mingled. The terrace looked down over a garden that
was a riot of colour; ruby-red hibiscus, bougainvillaea
and frangipani in every hue from palest amethyst to
flame-bright orange, and orchids growing like weeds
around the trunks of the trees. And in the air—
butterflies, hummingbirds, and tiny yellow-breasted
bananaquits.

Yes, the Blue Lagoon ought to be making a profit.
But the heavy repayments on the mortgages taken out
by Lauren's father and then by her husband were
crippling it. Would Joe be so keen to take it over if he
knew that? With a heavy thud of certainty she knew
that he would. Because Joe did not want the Blue
Lagoon only as an investment. As with many self-
made men, his pride now demanded that he should be
master where once he had been lackey.

Lauren could vividly recall the three years he had
spent there as manager, working long hard hours to
make the casino a success. He had seemed to have a
genuine liking and respect for her father, though it
was he who had borne the burden of his lethargy. But
after her marriage, Bill had quickly made himself very
unpopular with all the staff. It had been no surprise
that Joe had been the first to leave. After all that he
had put into the place, he had left with nothing; it was
understandable that he should cordially despise Bill
Henderson.

Joe Daley was a proud man. He had come from
nothing, and now he was one of the richest hoteliers in
the West Indies. If his methods might not bear close
scrutiny, there was no denying his success. And he had
only the best. His shirts were imported from Turnbull

and Asser in London, his wines came from the finest vineyards of France. His mistresses were the most beautiful women in the islands. And if he chose to take a wife, there was only one woman that people would agree was a worthy match for him: Lauren Henderson.

Though Lauren was not vain, neither was she blind to the covetous looks men cast at her, nor deaf to the legends that had grown up about her beauty. The cool façade behind which she had learned to hide her true emotions fascinated the gossip-loving visitors to the island. Though she did not quite like being the object of that sort of attention, she had to let herself be mildly amused by it. After all, it attracted customers to her establishment. Now that she was free to remarry, she knew that she could expect rivalry to break out among her admirers. But Joe Daley would brook no competition. He was a winner.

And now the uneasy peace between them had been shattered. The stakes had been called, and the game had begun in earnest. He had offered her marriage. She remembered that burning anger in his eyes when she had refused him. A frisson of fear made her hand shake. What would he do now? When Joe Daley wanted something, he got it.

Marry Joe? The idea might have its merits. A marriage of convenience, it would certainly be the end of all her financial worries. But even as the thought suggested itself, she rejected it. Joe Daley was not offering her the kind of sham marriage that Bill Henderson had tolerated after those first few terrible months. He wanted her, with a harsh masculine desire for possession, for ownership, for the satisfaction of appetites she had so innocently whetted seven years ago.

Memories swirled in her brain, stirring images that quickened her pulse . . .

'Mrs Henderson?' The voice came from a million miles away. 'Mrs Henderson, you asked to be informed if Mr Georgiou came near to losing ten thousand dollars. He's down nine-fifty, and playing deep.'

Lauren drew back painfully out of the smoked-honey heart of her glass, and glanced at her watch. It was almost four-thirty. Had she been sitting here dreaming for so long? Slipping from her stool, she parted the heavy bronze satin curtain and walked through into the hazy darkness of the gaming room. In the pools of green light that highlighted the remaining centres of interest, no head turned as she moved gracefully across the floor. Earlier in the evening nearly everyone would have looked up as she came in. But the low-stakes tables had closed down, and only the serious gamblers lingered.

The wealthy Greek businessman was bent over the roulette table, his eyes alight with that peculiar intensity that Lauren had come to recognise on sight. '*Rien ne va plus,*' called Lascelles, his voice nicely pitched to carry the length of his own table while not disturbing the concentration of the card players on the other side of the room. Mr Georgiou was riding the seventeen this time, and the white-lipped tension of his mouth revealed the strain he was under. He was wise to stick to roulette, Lauren thought wryly; he would be a lamb for the slaughter at poker.

Silently she moved behind him. The silver ball spun back, bounced, and settled. '*Dix-neuf,*' called Lascelles. 'Nineteen.' He flicked the rake over the table, drawing in the losing stakes, and the chips clacked quietly as he stacked them in the slot.

'Well, would you believe it?' muttered Mr Georgiou angrily. 'That's the third time the nineteen's come up in only twenty-two spins!' He watched forlornly as his piles of chips, so near yet so far away, were swept up by Lascelles' rake.

'Never mind, Mr Giorgiou. Perhaps you'll have better luck tomorrow.' Lauren's tone was sympathetic, but there was a thread of steel in it which carried a very definite warning. The little man rose indignantly to his feet, but under her cool gaze his anger stilled.

'Oh yes,' he said, trying to laugh, embarrassed. 'Of course, my dear. I have to try and win back some of my money.'

She smiled understandingly. 'If I might just mention it,' she murmured, so quietly that only he could hear, 'we would like time to clear your cheque before the tables open again. You understand, banking on these islands can be a little slow, and it can take all day to ring through to the mainland.'

A tinge of pink coloured his cheeks, but he said at once, 'Yes. Oh yes, of course, my dear. I'll see to it at once.'

'Please see Raoul,' she said smoothly. 'Good night, Mr Georgiou.'

'Good night. Oh, yes, good night, Mrs Henderson.' He was all affability now, and insisted on kissing her hand with extravagant gallantry. His eyes followed her as she walked from the room, but she had already forgotten him.

Harry was cashing up the bar till, and the last of the gamblers were drifting out of the casino. Lauren bade them a pleasant good night. Raoul came through with the casino takings, and he allowed himself a small smile of satisfaction.

'It's been a good night, Mrs Henderson,' he told her.

'I hope so, Raoul,' she told him frankly. 'I rather think we're going to need it.'

Raoul nodded, his dark face serious. 'If I may say so, Mrs Henderson, now that there will be fewer . . . expenses, I'm sure you will find that the profits will improve considerably.'

Lauren smiled wryly. Her late husband's lavish tastes had been a constant source of worry to her. But she had soon learned the futility of protesting. His gambling, his expensive private parties, the gee-gaws for his women, had been the price she had had to pay for being left alone.

With a smiling nod to her staff, who with the release of the evening's tension were laughing and chatting as they settled round the bar for their free last drink, Lauren carried the cashbox upstairs to her office overlooking the casino, and sat down at the big desk. This had been her routine nearly every night for seven years.

Swiftly adding up the receipts and mentally subtracting an estimate of running costs, she worked out how much she would be able to pay off the pile of debts that faced her—how much in a month, how much in a year. Without the drag of Bill's extravagance she would be able to turn a decent profit.

And one day, if she was lucky, she would be in the clear. Then she could start to run the place as she really wanted—and close down the casino. Though no one would have guessed it, she cordially despised some of the customers it attracted, and she hated presiding over gaming tables where the weak and foolish could be tempted into losing everything they had. One day she could close the casino, and run the place as a pleasant holiday resort, catering for water sports. One day.

With a sigh of satisfaction she stacked up the books and locked the money carefully in the big safe. Dawn was glimmering in the sky as she walked through the silent hotel to her private suite on the top floor. She crossed the sitting room quickly—it was still too redolent of the distasteful presence of her late husband.

In her own room, the one she had had since she was a baby, she undressed, and slipped a filmy wrap of French silk around her slim shoulders. Sitting at her elegant dressing table of gleaming rosewood, she took the pins from her hair and let it fall in a silken swathe down her back, and began to brush it with long sweeping strokes.

She was tired, but she was still too restless to sleep. The night time song of the tree-frogs was giving way to the piping chorus of see-sees and bananaquits, luring her out on to the balcony. No sign of life stirred in the boats lying quietly at anchor in the bay or tied up at the wooden jetty. The guest bungalows dotted about the bright gardens were silent and still. The sapphire waters of the lagoon barely rippled. Only the high crowns of the palms moved gently in the morning breeze from the sea.

Away to her left lay the forest of mangroves and bearded fig-trees that bordered the cultivated area of the Blue Lagoon. Beneath that tangle of greenery lay a hidden path. It led down to a secret cove, little more than a dent in the cliffs, with a tiny beach of powdery white sand. Lauren could still conjure the image of that beach just by closing her eyes. But she hadn't been down there for seven years.

CHAPTER TWO

IT was expected that the inquest would be routine, but Lauren guessed that it would attract a great deal of interest locally. The ordinary people of the islands savoured any scandal among the wealthy gambling socialites whose hedonistic lifestyle they both envied and condemned.

She dressed with care, knowing that whatever she wore would be subjected to the most critical scrutiny. She had chosen a very simple black suit, and had put her hair up in a severe style, but as she surveyed her reflection in the mirror she knew that she could not escape censure. The almost masculine lines of the suit only accentuated the feminine curves of her body, and the smooth sweep of her hair emphasised her lustrous eyes and the sensuous fullness of her lips. But glancing at her watch she knew it was too late to change. She lifted her head defiantly. Let them think what they liked. She had nothing to be ashamed of.

But as she walked down the stairs she suffered a shock that rocked her composure. Joe was waiting for her in the hall, dressed formally in a dark grey jacket and slim slacks of a paler grey, which he wore with a casual panache which underplayed the elegance of the tailoring. Lauren hesitated as he looked up at her appraisingly. 'Very chic,' he approved.

Her eyes flashed. 'It isn't supposed to be chic,' she snapped impatiently, walking past him.

He followed her, his long lazy stride effortlessly keeping pace with her brisk footsteps. His powerful cabin-cruiser, the *Midnight Lady*, was tied up alongside her own racy little motor-launch. She eyed it coldly.

'I assume you're planning to attend the inquest?' she enquired.

'I'm planning to escort you,' he responded with mocking gallantry.

'No, thank you.'

'You're thinking of your reputation?' he enquired sardonically. 'I assure you, sweetheart, you don't have one to lose.'

Her eyes blazed, but he calmly took her arm, and she was all too aware of the interested eyes watching from the other boats. She had no wish to entertain them by engaging in an undignified struggle with Joe, so flashing him a fulminating glance she allowed him to hand her aboard his boat.

She had been dreading the prospect of facing all those curious, speculative eyes at the inquest. At least Joe's presence would ensure that she was not openly insulted. But she knew only too well what would be whispered behind her back. Damn Joe Daley! she thought fiercely. Damn them all.

They didn't speak as the boat rode swiftly over the water to Kingstown, the capital of St Vincent and the administrative centre of the Northern Grenadines. It was only a short distance from the quayside to the Coroner's court. A small knot of people had gathered around the entrance, and Lauren caught her breath, her footsteps faltering.

'Come along, sweetheart. Into the lions' den,' murmured Joe, taking her elbow and propelling her forward.

The crowd parted to let them through, and closed in behind them. Every head turned as they walked to their seats at the front of the small courtroom. Lauren

tilted her head at a proud angle, though her spine felt
as if it were made of ice that was slowly melting in the
heat of the stares that were burning into her back.

'The court will rise.'

The Coroner took his place, and surveyed the
courtroom with a serious but kindly gaze. 'This is an
inquest, not a trial,' he announced in a voice that
carried effortlessly to the back of the public benches,
'but it is a court of law and must be respected
accordingly.' He referred to the papers on his desk.
'We are here to enquire into the death of Mr William
Roosevelt Lincoln Henderson, late of the Blue Lagoon
Hotel, on the island of St Arnoux, in the district of the
Northern Grenadines. Do we have formal notice of
identification?'

Lauren listened abstractedly to the ponderous
official statements. A slight buzz rose behind her as
Bill's date of birth was read out. It hadn't taken people
long to work out that he had been nearly thirty years
older than her. But such arrangements were not
uncommon among the super-rich jet-setters who
cruised the islands.

She risked a careful glance at Joe's impassive
profile. He had been painfully close to the truth when
he had accused her father of selling her to the highest
bidder. Poor Dad! He had thought he was securing her
future. Before he had died he had had to face the fact
that his scheme had misfired. Bill Henderson had been
no millionaire; merely a hanger-on, with a private
income just large enough to buy him a few luxuries
with which to impress. But at least Dad had never
known the worst.

The proceedings plodded on—all the sordid details of
Bill's lifestyle, of a marriage that had been hell, all the
things that Lauren had tried to hide for so long—were

being dissected by the Coroner's precise questioning, laid out like dry bones to be picked over by the curious.

She held her head erect, aware of the occasional murmurs behind her, aware of Joe sitting motionless beside her. Why had he insisted on escorting her? It was as if he had chosen to stake his claim to her in the most public way. Idly she twirled the wedding ring that she had not yet bothered to take off.

Poor, pathetic Bill. However much she had despised him, she could never have dreamed that he would come to such a trifling end. He had drowned in the floodlit swimming-pool, in full view of all his wastrel friends. He had been throwing one of his wild parties, and he'd dived into the pool, fully dressed. Drunk—of course. They had all thought he was fooling around when he had floated to the surface, face down, arms outstretched. They had stood around, shrieking with laughter, calling out wittily to him, until someone had noticed a trickle of blood, and screamed. He had dived in at the shallow end, and knocked himself out, and drowned as they all stood watching.

The verdict was 'Misadventure'. The court adjourned, and the babble of voices rose from the crowded public benches. Lauren took a deep breath, and stood up. A sea of faces confronted her, seemingly impenetrable; most mildly curious, a few self-righteously hostile. A couple of reporters surged towards her, a flashlight dazzled her eyes, and she flinched away instinctively. At once Joe's arm came round her shoulders, protectively, possessively, sweeping her through the crowd and out into the street.

'Mrs Henderson, why weren't you at the party that night?' one of the reporters called out, darting along behind them. 'Who were you with? How much money do you stand to inherit in your husband's will?'

She hurried along, head down, ducking into the safety of Joe's encircling arm. She knew which picture was going to be in the papers tomorrow. The beautiful young widow in the arms of her lover at the inquest on her wealthy husband. The kind of salacious stuff the newspapers loved, and no one would believe for a moment that she was innocent.

As soon as they were clear of the harbour she turned her rage on Joe. 'Well?' she demanded in cold fury. 'Are you satisfied? You know what they'll all be saying now!'

He shrugged his wide shoulders indifferently. 'Why should you care what they say?'

'Not care? The scandalmongers will be having a field day.'

'They've been saying for years that we're lovers,' he answered, quite unruffled. 'They'll have plenty more to say about you after this morning's choice revelations.'

'Not if you hadn't been there,' she retorted, struggling to control her temper. 'I've done nothing to be ashamed of.'

'The perfect little wife,' he mocked sarcastically. 'Such a pity to waste all that loyalty on an evil little slug like Bill Henderson!'

'It isn't fair to insult him now he's dead,' she flashed.

His dark eyes held hers. 'Why go on pretending, Lauren?' he asked. 'It can't have been much of a marriage.' She turned away from him sharply. 'And now you're free,' he added softly.

'It doesn't make the slightest difference,' she said stiffly. 'I have no intention of marrying again.'

'No?' He had set the auto-pilot, and Lauren tensed as she sensed his approach.

'Don't you touch me,' she warned in a voice that would strip paint.

He was standing behind her, maybe twelve inches away from her, but she could feel a potent electrical charge tingling across the gap. She gripped the rail, her knuckles white.

'Why go on fighting it, Lauren?' His voice was huskily seductive. 'I can feel your body's hunger. You know I can give you what you need.'

Lauren's heart was pounding so fast she felt dizzy. 'Oh, your lines are beautiful, Joe,' she said a little shakily, 'but I'm not going to fall for them this time.' She took a deep, steadying breath. 'I suppose you'll be telling me next that you're in love with me,' she challenged mockingly.

His laugh was chilling. 'I wouldn't insult your intelligence,' he sneered.

'Then why do you want to marry me?' she asked coldly.

He moved forward, trapping her against the rail, and his hands gripped her slender waist, holding her hard against him. His voice was harsh in her ear. 'Do I have to spell it out?' he demanded roughly. 'I've waited too long to be content with just having you in my bed for a few nights, Lauren. I'm going to own you. I'm going to write my name all over you.' He forced her to turn round, and his face hovered inches above hers. 'I'll punish you for every extra hour you make me wait,' he warned. 'You know I'm going to win in the end.'

Lauren summoned every ounce of resistance into her voice. 'Oh no, you're not!' she parried viciously.

'Aren't I?' He lifted his hand, and laid it along her cheek. His thumb brushed across her lips, parting them a little. His eyes scorched down into hers. 'We'll see.' Abruptly he turned away from her, and walked back to the helm, such arrogance in his step that she longed to throw something at him.

Two days later the funeral was held. It was a sad funeral in its way. Nothing and no one in the whole world seemed to care that Bill Henderson was dead. The sun shone indifferently in the high bright sky, the birds trilled cheerfully in the waving heads of the jacarandas. He was laid to rest with only his widow to bid him a last farewell. Lauren stood at the graveside, glad of the black veil across her face to hide the lack of emotion in her eyes.

From the shadow of the church two elderly parishioners, who had come to put flowers on the altar, watched the solemn proceedings.

'That's Lauren Holding, as was,' clucked one, 'the one whose father drunk himself to death.'

'Now her poor husband's gone and done the same thing,' the other added disapprovingly.

'They say,' the first confided in a low tone, 'that she was drinking champagne with her lover the very night her husband died.'

The two old crones exchanged significant glances, and hurried back into the safety of the church before the evil woman should turn and look towards them.

The vicar recited the service, a little embarrassed by the poor attendance. The coffin was lowered, and the widow threw a small posy of violets down on to it, then stepped back from the graveside and lifted the neat veil from her face. She turned to the vicar and smiled. 'Thank you for the service,' she said. 'It was very dignified.'

Her voice was low and melodious. For all that people said of her, he reflected, his impression was only one of serenity and charm. Though she had the finest eyes he had ever seen. 'Won't you stay for tea?' he enquired politely.

'Thank you, but no. I have some business to attend to before I return to St Arnoux.' Lauren extended one elegant hand, and he shook it, and watched as she turned and walked gracefully down the drive.

The sidewalk was shaded from the hot Caribbean sun by wide brick arcades, and as she threaded her way through the milling shoppers and strollers someone fell into step beside her. 'Good afternoon, Joe,' she said without glancing at him. 'I had no idea that you mourned my husband's death so much as to wish to attend his funeral.'

'I mourn him as much as you do, sweetheart,' he responded laconically.

'I'm not sure that I'm quite in the mood for your cynicism today, Joe,' she snapped acidly. 'Nor, to be frank, your company.'

'Such claws!' he chided gently. 'You're like a panther—a sleek black panther.' She flashed him a freezing glance, but met only mocking amusement. 'It'll be fun to tame you,' he added, his voice deceptively soft, 'you'll purr like a kitten.'

'Panthers eat live meat,' she threw at him. 'Be careful I don't turn on you.'

'Do you think you could?' he challenged mockingly.

'I shan't bother to try,' she returned, an inflection of cool indifference in her voice. 'I'm fussy who I eat.'

'Poor Bill—I almost begin to feel sorry for him.'

'You always despised him,' she rapped tartly.

'Of course. He was a weak, gluttonous fool, but he had what I wanted.'

'Me, or the Blue Lagoon?' she enquired coldly.

His hard mouth curved into a taunting smile. 'Both,

little kitten,' he told her, an unmistakable thread of menace in his voice. 'You should really give my offer serious consideration while you have the chance, you know.'

'It really doesn't interest me,' she returned loftily. 'The Blue Lagoon isn't for sale, and nor am I.'

He laughed, sending an icy shiver scudding down her spine. 'Ah, you still have plenty of spirit,' he approved teasingly.

Lauren stopped walking, and looked up at him, her eyes signalling danger. 'I thought I'd made it plain that I want nothing to do with you, Joe,' she snapped. 'If you were half a gentleman . . .'

'Ah, but I never pretended to be a gentleman,' he returned, deliberately provocative. 'And you certainly aren't a lady!' Her hand swung, but he caught it long before it could strike that arrogant face. 'Oh no, little kitten,' he scolded, 'that's very uncivilised. You have a lot to learn.' His eyes glinted satanically as he turned her hand over, and with mocking gallantry kissed her trembling fingers. 'I look forward to the pleasure of teaching you. But for now, *au revoir*,' he murmured, and then he was gone, dodging across the road between the rushing traffic with the supreme self-confidence of one who has been assured by the gods that nothing could touch him.

He moved with a lithe, animal grace, his athletic build underlined by the casual shirt and close-fitting jeans he was wearing. Lauren stared after him, her mind in turmoil. Why had he come? He had had no intention of attending the funeral—his clothes stated that plainly. Was he spying on her, perhaps guessing at the nature of the 'other business' she had to attend to? But then why would he make his presence known to her? To make her nervous, perhaps?

He had succeeded in that, she acknowledged ruefully. She could not shake off the apprehension that she was still being watched. Did he hope to frighten her into surrendering before the fight had even begun? He had underestimated her, she vowed resolutely. Pride lifted her head as she opened the door of the rather scruffy offices of the man who had conducted her late husband's business affairs.

This was not a meeting that she was looking forward to with any degree of pleasure, but it was best to get it over with as soon as possible. Alec McGuiness was a thin, anxious-looking man. He flustered around his cluttered little office, shifting piles of documents from here to there so that he could offer Lauren a place to sit. He really looked as if he would be more at home with simple things like motor insurance brokerage than with the investment side of the business. It was hard to see why Bill had employed him. But then, perhaps not. Bill would not have tolerated anyone who might criticise some of his more harebrained schemes, or indeed who appeared in any way more intelligent than himself. He had probably settled on McGuiness after transferring his business from every broker in the islands.

'My dear Mrs Henderson, so very pleasant to see you! I'm only sad that it should be in such tragic circumstances,' he fluttered. 'I was terribly upset at the news, you know. I thought of your poor husband as one of my dearest friends, as well as a valued client. I was absolutely stunned to hear of his death. I would have come to the funeral, but . . . well, I feel such sad occasions are best left to the family. But now, my dear,' he beamed, 'let me say that I do hope you will allow me to be of service to you as I was to poor Bill.'

Lauren eyed him doubtfully as she sat down. His

breathless little speech had done nothing to improve her opinion of him. 'Mr McGuiness, I am the sole beneficiary under my husband's will,' she began without preamble. 'His trust fund ceases on his death. That leaves only his investments.'

Mr McGuiness coughed nervously. 'But Mrs Henderson, there are no investments,' he said. 'I'm afraid poor Bill sold out his few remaining Government Bonds last year.'

That was a disappointment, but she hadn't expected much. 'Then that leaves only the mortgages for us to discuss,' she continued calmly.

'Ah yes. The mortgages and the other loans.'

'Other loans?'

He smiled waveringly, and pulled a thick portfolio from his drawer. 'Over the past few years your husband has been running quite heavily into debt, I'm afraid. But not all of them are secured against the Blue Lagoon,' he added as if it were a reassurance. But since the only capital, the only income, she had was entirely tied up in the Blue Lagoon it made little difference, Lauren mused wryly. 'Some of the loans were at rather a high rate of interest, you see,' he went on apologetically. 'They were originally intended to be only short-term. There was a hundred thousand dollars to buy his yacht, the *Yellow Rose*.'

'But he sold her the following year. Didn't he pay off the loan?'

'I'm afraid not. Then there was another quarter of a million to invest in the Port Elizabeth Petroleum Company. I'm afraid he didn't get the return he expected on that.'

Lauren looked at him suspiciously. 'He told me he invested only fifty thousand,' she said. Silently he handed her a sheaf of papers. Two hundred and fifty thousand dollars borrowed at fifteen per cent compound interest, twenty-five thousand useless shares. It was irrefutable. 'Weren't you supposed to be his financial adviser?' she demanded impatiently. 'How could you let him be so foolish?'

The little man shifted uncomfortably, his eyes not meeting hers. 'It could have been an excellent investment,' he defended weakly. 'If they'd found oil, he could have got a return of a hundred, even a hundred and fifty per cent in a couple of years.'

' "If",' she commented acidly. She sighed, and leaned back in her chair, crossing her long legs elegantly. 'Perhaps you'd better go through the whole batch and tell me what I owe to whom,' she suggested wearily. It took some time; there were far more of them than she'd anticipated. 'I've never heard of most of these companies,' she said when he had finished. She picked up one of the contracts, and glanced at it. 'Straker Investments,' she read. 'Who are they?'

'They're a Chicago-based company. A very good firm,' Alec McGuiness assured her confidently.

She raised an enquiring eyebrow. 'Have you read their penalty clauses?' she enquired dryly.

He took the document back from her quickly. 'Yes . . . well . . .' he flustered.

'How far are the payments in default?' she insisted.

'That one? Oh . . . only a couple of months.'

'At an extra two per cent interest? I seem to be in a worse position than I thought. What about the others? Are they as bad?'

'Not all of them.' He tried to smile, but met a glacial stare.

'How much, exactly, do I have to pay each month to keep all these loans up to date?' she asked in a clipped voice. He told her, and she was betrayed into a most unladylike utterance. She would have to give up a few little luxuries—like eating!

'If you'll take my advice, Mrs Henderson,' said McGuiness, sitting forward and speaking in a low, confidential tone, 'you'll sell the place.'

'Sell it?'

He nodded gravely. 'I can get you a good price. Enough to cover nearly all your debts.'

'You mean that even if I sold the Blue Lagoon, I would still owe money?' Only years of self-discipline enabled her to keep her voice steady.

'Well . . . yes,' he admitted reluctantly.

'Then I won't sell. I can make enough profit to pay off the loans,' she stated with a confidence she did not feel.

'I'm afraid it might not be as simple as that,' he said, his eyes evading hers again.

'And what is that supposed to mean?' she enquired frostily.

'You see, some of your creditors may feel that a woman couldn't run a casino successfully on her own,' he explained a trifle sheepishly. 'They may prefer to have their money back at once.'

'I see. Well, I'll just have to prove them wrong, won't I?' she responded briskly. 'If I can keep up the payments, they won't be able to do anything about it.'

'Mrs Henderson, I'm not talking about your friendly local bank manager,' he insisted nervously. 'These people are from the States. Why don't you get out while you can?'

Lauren stood up, extending her hand coolly to shake his clammy one. 'I think I've made my position quite clear, Mr McGuiness,' she said decisively. 'I will not sell the Blue Lagoon. Please let me have a full account of my commitments. Good afternoon.'

CHAPTER THREE

THE small port of Kingstown was bustling with life. Donkey carts vied with noisy diesel lorries to transport their wares down to the deep-water harbour. An ocean-going cargo vessel was being crane-loaded with sacks of arrowroot, while nearer at hand an elderly island schooner was being stacked with bananas by a group of singing women in bright batik-printed dresses and head-scarves.

Lauren gazed round the wide shallow sweep of the bay, set among its tree-clad hills, feeling a surge of affection. She had been born in a small private hospital here in the capital of St Vincent. She had attended a boarding school just outside the town. She knew that the shops were not as good as those in Bridgetown, Barbados, and that the harbour was not considered to be as picturesque as St George on Grenada, at the southern end of the Grenadines chain. But she loved the delightful shabbiness of the arcaded streets.

She knew all the history of the island—how the fierce Carib indians had defied the might of the British and French for years, making it a haven for those displaced by the colonisation of other islands, and for runaway slaves; how the British had gradually achieved supremacy, crowned by the building of Fort Charlotte, six hundred feet up on Berkshire Hill to the north-west of town.

She could have been a tourist guide, if the island had been more of a magnet for visitors. But St Vincent

was poor and underdeveloped, and the few visitors
who came were there for the sun and the sea, isolated
in their luxury resorts, not interested in seeing the
sights. She stood little chance of finding work here if
she lost the Blue Lagoon.

She gazed bleakly out over the shining water. She
stood little chance of finding honest work anywhere if
she lost the Blue Lagoon. She had no family—some
distant cousins in Caracas that she'd never seen, and
an even more remote aunt of her father's living in
England. If she was forced to sell up, she had few
illusions about the sort of life that lay before her. The
only thing she knew was running a nightclub. But
though for a beautiful woman a nightclub job would
be easy to find, it would not be as manager. And virtue
was cheap in the playground of the rich.

Repressing a shudder, she strolled on down to the
quayside, where her own swift little motor-launch was
moored. She would have to trade in the *Petrel* for a
much cheaper boat, of course . . . But no, on second
thoughts, she'd keep her. She had to present the
illusion that all was well. If she let herself be panicked
into revealing just how serious her financial position
really was, her creditors would be on her like a pack of
wolves.

She nudged the boat carefully out of the crowded
harbour. McGuiness's words were revolving in her
brain. She needed time. Time to prove to her creditors
that she could run the casino on her own and meet all
her commitments. Then would they leave her alone?
How long would it take to convince them? She
clenched her fist fiercely. She'd fight them, whoever
they were. She had no choice. And one day she'd be
free of them, and Coconut Beach would be truly her
own. One day.

The nightclub was reassuringly busy again. A steel band was playing, and couples were dancing. The supper room was full, and at the gaming tables money was flowing into her coffers. Lauren sat at her usual place at the end of the bar, sipping her iced Perrier water. She was wearing black again—a sleek halter-necked dress of subtly shimmering satin that skimmed her slender curves and fell in a slim line to the floor. Her hair was elegantly upswept, and diamonds sparkled in her ears.

She was aware of the interest that surrounded her. Now that her husband was dead, gossip was rife about what she would do. She knew that she was popularly credited with having a number of lovers, chief among them being Joe Daley. Now that she was free, would she marry Joe? The question was in everyone's eyes.

Joe Daley was either unaware of the speculation about his intentions towards the beautiful widow, or he was unconcerned. Those who knew him were inclined to believe the latter. Whatever the truth, he gave the scandalmongers the finest fuel by breaking with his usual custom and visiting the Blue Lagoon twice in one week.

'Well,' remarked Lauren dryly as he seated himself casually beside her at the bar, 'we are honoured. What's the matter? Has Hurricane Bay run out of rye?'

'Nothing so serious,' he drawled with that devastating smile as Harry placed a thick tumbler of rye whisky at his elbow, 'I came over to ask you to marry me again.'

'I'm so glad it was nothing important,' she murmured sweetly.

'I felt I might have been a little hasty the other night,' he went on, quite unruffled, 'but now that the funeral is over there can be no possible risk of scandal.'

'That would be a reassuring thought if I felt remotely inclined to accept your offer.'

Despite the lightness of his tone, there was a dangerous glint in his eyes as he said, 'Look on it as a business proposition, sweetheart. This is a very small island. Why compete for trade?'

'Oh, Joe!' she exclaimed in spurious sympathy, 'I had no idea you were in financial trouble. Can I lend you a few dollars out of the till?'

He laughed, but his eyes held no trace of amusement. 'It isn't me that's in trouble, sweetheart,' he returned. 'You're mortgaged up to your big beautiful eyes.'

Lauren's mind was racing. Had he bullied Mr McGuiness into giving him confidential information about her affairs? He could just be probing, but if he knew a little of the truth he would never believe an outright denial that she was in debt. It might be better to try to make him believe that the situation was not really serious.

She play-acted a heartfelt sigh, her eyes dancing to tell him that she was teasing. 'I know,' she admitted with a sigh. 'Such a waste of effort to marry a millionaire if he only goes and spends all his money on himself.'

'Ah, I see,' nodded Joe in cynical amusement. 'Then your maidenly reluctance on this occasion doesn't stem from any distaste for the contract I'm offering, but from a fear that I might not honour my side of the deal? Don't worry, sweetheart. You'll be able to get your sticky little fingers on a reasonable amount of my worldly goods.'

'Oh no, Joe,' she countered with nice distaste, 'such dirty money!'

His eyes flashed with momentary anger, swiftly masked. 'Most of your money comes from gambling too,' he pointed out smoothly. 'Or do you subscribe to the local rumour that I'm hand-in-glove with the Mafia?'

Lauren was startled that he should issue such a blunt challenge. 'Are you?' she asked, trying to read the truth in the unfathomable darkness of his eyes. He returned her searching gaze levelly, but gave her no answer.

She was the first to look away, her heart fluttering wildly. She had never really believed that Joe could be directly involved in anything criminal. And yet where had he been those four missing years, and how had he made the money to buy Hurricane Bay? She had heard rumours, of course—most of them probably highly exaggerated. He was said to have been smuggling drugs into North America, or arms into Central America. Since his return, no one had actually had the nerve to ask him.

Covertly she studied his face. It had changed little in seven years; a suggestion of grey at the temples, a little more leanness beneath the stone-carved cheek-bones. There had always been a certain hardness about his level mouth, but the eyes used to smile at her—long ago. Now they regarded her with a cynical speculation that infuriated her. Marry him? What a preposterous idea!

She smiled coolly. 'There are always so many rumours, Joe, one really doesn't know what to believe.'

'Doesn't one?' he mocked.

She felt her temper rising. No one else could make her angry so easily as Joe could. 'Well, it's your own fault if people talk about you,' she snapped. 'I think you like having a shady past!'

He turned his eyes towards her, holding her prisoner with his level gaze. 'They talk about you too, Lauren,' he said, his voice warm velvet over cold steel. 'They say you've had dozens of lovers since your marriage.'

She could feel a slow blush creeping up over her cheeks, but she could not escape that searching gaze. 'It isn't true,' she whispered tensely.

'Isn't it?'

She shook her head, her eyes never leaving his. He seemed to be plundering the very depths of her soul. And then abruptly he released her, leaving her feeling shattered, ravaged. 'Anyway, even if I had, it wouldn't be any of your business,' she protested belatedly. He raised one eyebrow in sardonic amusement. 'I'm not going to marry you. You're wasting your time,' she declared breathlessly.

'Oh, I don't think so,' he drawled, calmly sipping his drink. 'Hunting panthers wouldn't be nearly so much fun if they came straight to hand like tame pussycats.'

Lauren's self-control snapped. With an angry exclamation she swished through the curtain into the gaming room. She stood for several seconds surveying the players until her breathing steadied and her heartbeat returned to normal. Then with her mask carefully restored she moved forward to stroll discreetly among the tables, ensuring that everything was running smoothly.

It was another good night, but she was too wise to set much store by that. It was only to be expected that there would also be occasional setbacks. Mr Georgiou was at the roulette table again, his credit fully restored. A flashy young Texan was trying to stake above the limit clearly indicated by the notice on the wall above Lascelles' head. She caught Lascelles' eye, and silently drew his attention to the problem.

'*Pardon, Monsieur*. You have staked above the limit,' Lascelles pointed out to him with exceeding politeness.

'That's okay. Let it ride,' the Texan drawled loudly.

Lauren stepped up to the table. 'I'm sorry, sir, I cannot allow you to stake that amount,' she said quietly. It was a rule that protected both the casino and the punter, some of whom would double their stake time after time if allowed to do so.

The Texan laughed. 'What's up, sugar? Afraid of losing to me?'

'I'm sorry, sir,' she repeated patiently, 'it's against the rules of the casino.'

'Ah, come on, baby! Where's your sense of adventure? Rules were made to be broken,' he protested. His voice was a little slurred, and Lauren realised that he was rather drunk. She hoped there was not going to be an unpleasant scene; this was exactly the sort of situation that people would say a woman couldn't handle. That she had coped with scores of drunks with no support from her husband would be forgotten. If she made a mistake with this one, it would be said to prove the point.

But unexpectedly the man backed down, and removed his chips. Lauren glanced over her shoulder to see Joe standing there, one hand casually in his pocket, but his eyes fixed on the troublemaker in unmistakable warning. He didn't have to say a word. No one argued with Joe Daley.

Lauren felt an irrational surge of annoyance. 'Thank you,' she snapped acidly. 'But it really wasn't necessary for you to intervene.'

'I'm sure it wasn't,' he agreed, a quirk of amusement in his voice.

'Everything was perfectly under control,' she added, tilting her head at a haughty angle.

'I'm sure it was,' he responded blandly.

'I'm perfectly capable of looking after my own affairs.'

'I'm glad to hear it.'

Lauren stalked from the room, furious with herself for letting him get under her skin. She circulated round the nightclub, talking pleasantly with her guests, even delighting some of the men by consenting to dance with them. But all the time she was aware of Joe, at the stool next to hers at the bar, waiting for her like a patient hunter.

She could not avoid him all night, so at last, with a tense little quiver of apprehension, she returned to the bar. He acknowledged her with a faint quizzical gleam. 'Everything still under control?' he taunted sardonically.

'Yes, thank you,' she responded coolly.

One dark eyebrow lifted fractionally. 'Still determined to try to run the place on your own?' he enquired.

'Yes, I am,' she returned, her voice betraying a little of her tension.

'You know, I have a very special interest in the Blue Lagoon,' he murmured silkily, 'so if you should ever find yourself in difficulties . . .'

'Thank you, but I can take care of myself,' she retorted sharply.

'Gambling can be a very risky business.'

'I'm not a gambler,' she stated calmly. 'I calculate the odds, and I never take on more than I can handle.'

Joe smiled slowly. 'Then I don't suppose you'd dare to play cards with me?' he challenged.

Lauren hesitated. She didn't want to admit that she

was afraid she couldn't handle him. She shrugged her slender shoulders in calculated indifference. 'The casino's fairly quiet. I could spare an hour or two for a game,' she conceded coolly.

'Canasta?'

She inclined her head in assent, and led him through into the gaming room. To one side there were several small tables, suitable for private games. Green leather chairs, high-backed and pivot-sprung, ensured the players' comfort, and lights shaded with green silk hung low to bathe the baize playing-top with restful light.

Raoul brought two packs of cards, and Lauren handed them to Joe to break the seals. 'How much shall we play for?' he asked.

'Dollar points?' she suggested rather recklessly.

He lifted an eyebrow in mocking derision. 'Ah, come on,' he drawled, 'why don't we add a little savour to the game?'

Icy fingers began to curl around Lauren's heart, but her smile was tranquil. 'You are my guest,' she told him graciously. 'Please name your stakes.'

'Shall we say ten-dollar points?' he suggested.

'Certainly.' She didn't even blink. So he planned to go straight for the jugular? The potential stakes in the game were fifty thousand dollars! Though she was confident that she couldn't lose more than ten thousand, even that amount would certainly wreck any hope she had of satisfying her creditors.

Did Joe know that? *Had* he bullied McGuiness into revealing how close she was to financial disaster? Had he deliberately lured her into this game with the intention of ruining her, knowing that without the tempting dowry of the Blue Lagoon to offer, most of her other suitors would quickly bow out of the scene?

And then, bankrupt and helpless, she would have little choice but to accept whatever offer he chose to make, for herself and for the Blue Lagoon.

But not one hint of these anxious thoughts showed in her cool dark eyes as she skilfully shuffled the two packs of cards together and slid them across the table for Joe to cut. He cut a ten, but Lauren turned up a queen. 'Your deal, sweetheart,' he told her with a lazy smile.

Lauren stacked the cards and began to deal. Her first hand was quite a good one, but at that early stage of the game a good deal of luck was involved. She won the hand, but Joe had scored more points, and it was points that counted.

Joe dealt the second hand, and when Lauren picked up her cards she had to suppress a surge of pure delight. Luck had certainly smiled on her this time! But she hid her elation carefully, playing her turns steadily until she had completed her hand, and could lay her cards for a concealed win, catching Joe by surprise. She couldn't resist a triumphant smile.

'Well done,' he congratulated her, leaning back in his seat, 'I didn't see that coming.' He was smiling, but his eyes were watching her intently, aware now of just how well she could conceal her thoughts.

'I had some lucky cards,' she responded cautiously.

Joe sighed, feigning despondency. 'Maybe I'd better start cheating after all,' he drawled.

'Oh, I don't think you need to start panicking just yet,' she returned sweetly. 'The game's hardly begun.'

Again that deep, velvety laugh. 'It's a long time since we played together,' he said softly, his voice adding hidden layers to his meaning. 'I'd almost forgotten how much I enjoyed it.'

Lauren was glad she had to concentrate on her deal.

A small knot of spectators was gathering around them, intrigued by the battle between these two who had been the subject of so much gossip for so many years. Lauren didn't care to be the centre of attention in this way, but she would not allow it to distract her. She knew that she needed all her concentration for the game. In spite of her two wins, Joe was ahead on points. His memory was phenomenal, and his assessment of the cards she was holding seemed quite diabolical. She tried varying her discard policy to confuse him, but ended up ruining her hand and losing heavily.

Joe sipped his rye whisky slowly. The alcohol was in no way fogging his brain, she thought crossly. Under his contemplative gaze she fluffed her adding up, and had to count her score again. But on the next hand he needed more points to open, and that gave her the advantage she needed to catch up a little. As she totted up her points and found that they amounted to nearly four thousand she felt a surge of relief. Even if Joe won every game, she couldn't lose more than ten thousand dollars now, at the worst. She sipped her iced Perrier water, her face serene.

The crowd around them had grown, and there was a considerable amount of side-betting on the result. Most seemed to be backing Joe, and he smiled across the table at Lauren. There was something tigerish in that smile, and Lauren felt like a small mouse between the paws of a very clever cat.

'It looks as if I'm odds-on favorite,' he drawled laconically.

'So it seems,' she returned, unruffled.

'Why don't we have a little wager on the outcome ourselves?' he suggested with a twist of amusement. 'Evens, of course.'

'Why not?' she returned, her heart thumping.

'Shall we say . . . ten thousand dollars?'

Lauren felt vaguely sick. 'By all means,' she answered with an untroubled smile. She shuffled the cards, her hands miraculously steady. The crowd was pressing in around her, making her feel trapped. Joe had a way of looking at her that made her feel half-naked, and she wished the black dress did not mould the curves of her body quite so intimately. Joe looked immaculate, as usual, his elegantly-styled white dinner jacket perfectly moulding his wide shoulders. His crisp white shirt was flawless. Lauren found herself wondering who took care of his clothes.

She was forced to pull herself together and direct her attention to her cards. She did not have a good hand, but if she built patiently . . . Ten thousand dollars! Why on earth had she agreed? She must be crazy! If she lost that much . . . She took another sip of Perrier to counter the dryness of her mouth.

'Are you warm?' asked Joe, that slow smile mocking her.

'A little.' She glanced swiftly at her watch. It was after midnight.

Joe laid the jack of spades on the discard pack. She had a pair in her hand, but she couldn't remember what other cards had already been laid. Damn her wandering attention! She hesitated, unsure. Joe's face was impassive, but there was a stir round the table. Impulsively she laid her cards, and picked up the pack.

She knew she'd made a bad mistake as soon as she looked at the cards she held. She'd left herself in the unenviable position of having little chance of winning the hand, and she would have to discard to Joe with very limited scope for strategy. She knew by his bland expression that he was taking pleasure in her discomfort.

He exploited her vulnerability to the full. Every point he scored felt like another nail in her coffin. 'It looks like you're not doing too well, sweetheart,' he drawled, lifting his whisky glass to his lips.

'I do seem to be having a bad hand,' she agreed with studied nonchalance. She cast her eyes along the array of cards he had spread before him. There was almost nothing she could discard now without adding to his points, while her own score was paltry. If fortune had been kind to her she could have drawn the cards she needed, but the devil was smiling on his own. The cards danced before her like imps luring her on to her own destruction. If only she had never got herself into this!

Inevitably, the cards that were left in her hand as the game wore on were all cards that would benefit Joe's score. Finally she could do nothing but give him a card that would complete a Canasta set, worth valuable bonus points. With a wry smile she drew it from her hand and laid it on the discard pack.

A murmur ran round the audience. Only Joe showed no reaction; no triumph, no gloating, nothing. He simply stretched out his hand and picked up the cards. Calmly he stacked the Canasta set, and laid out the rest of his cards, until he held only two in his hand. Only then did he permit himself a smile.

'I think you're losing, sweetheart,' he remarked. Lauren clamped her teeth into the softness of her lower lip in a vain effort to stop it trembling. 'You can't afford to lose that much, can you?' he asked quietly.

She took a deep, steadying breath. 'I haven't lost yet,' she pointed out in a voice of commendable calm.

He laughed, low in his throat, and then with calculated deliberation he laid a joker on to another pile of cards, stacked them into a second Canasta set, and discarded his remaining card. His eyes caught hers and held them trapped. 'Ah, but you have lost,' he said in that husky-soft voice that touched her tightly drawn nerve fibres like a bow across the strings of a cello.

A sigh, of congratulation, of sympathy, of tension released, rippled round the spectators. Lauren looked down at her cards. She had barely two hundred points. There was a pain in her chest as if someone had stuck a knife into her. She had lost more than eighteen thousand dollars. Blindly she reached for her glass, but the chinking of the ice betrayed the shaking of her hand, so she put it down again.

'I'm prepared to write off your losses,' Joe said quietly. His eyes drifted slowly downwards, lingering over the curves of her body in a way that added a hint of audacious significance to his words.

A whisper rose around the table. Lauren stared at him dumbly, knowing that he could read in her eyes the desperation that she could not hide. But surely he wouldn't dare . . . She felt her cheeks blush a heated scarlet. In a voice that shook uncontrollably she spoke to her head croupier, who had moved discreetly to her side. 'Raoul, fetch me the cashbox.'

'I don't want your money,' said Joe calmly.

'You go too far . . .' she whispered angrily.

His dark eyes were glinting with mockery. Even as the thought flashed through her brain to throw her drink at him she found her wrist pinned to the table. Her flesh burned as if his fingers were hot steel. 'I don't want your money,' he repeated. 'There's something else I'll take in lieu of my winnings.'

'Sir, your terms are insulting!' she spat at him.

He lifted one satanic eyebrow in sardonic amusement, and as she gazed at him helplessly across the
table he raised his hand to her cheek. She gasped, and
saw her diamond earring sparkling in his fingers.

'I'll take this,' he said, 'on one condition. That you
play me for the other one. At my place.' He dropped
the earring into his pocket. A ripple of applause went
round the audience. Lauren's heart was beating so fast
she was afraid she would faint. The fingers that had
gripped her wrist moved, and lifted her hand, and his
lips brushed lightly across her fingers. 'Shall we say
the day after tomorrow?' he murmured, and then he
was gone, vanishing out of the pool of light so
suddenly that to Lauren's misted eyes he seemed like
the devil incarnate.

A babble of conversation rose around her, and the
crowd began to melt away. Lauren sat for a moment
where she was, unwilling to trust her legs.

'Shall I put the cashbox away, Mrs Henderson?'
came Raoul's soft voice, drawing her back to reality.

'Oh . . . no, I'll take it up, thank you, Raoul,' she
answered. She stood up slowly, and clutching the
heavy box in her arms like a shield, she walked across
the room and up the stairs to her office. She was aware
of a new interest in the eyes of the men as they
watched her. Every one of them believed that Joe had
offered her eighteen thousand dollars to openly
become his mistress. He had been playing to the
gallery, deliberately fuelling the intrigue that surrounded them. He had certainly raised the stakes
again, she thought wryly. If she continued to hold out
against what was becoming a siege there was no telling
what he might do. As if she didn't have enough to
worry about, she thought angrily as she shut the

cashbox into the safe, without Joe Daley trying to seduce her!

It was only then that she remembered that the diamond earring was fake. In the secluded quiet of the office she began to laugh. Weakly she leaned against the desk, tears streaming down her face, shaking with what she realised was almost hysteria.

CHAPTER FOUR

THE afternoon was as nearly perfect as any afternoon could be. A soft zephyr breeze blew from the warm sea, just enough to dance with the orchids and oleanders. On the sapphire waters of the bay, shining white sails tacked to and fro.

Lauren lay on a striped sun-lounger on one corner of the terrace, sipping her favourite sparkling mineral water and surveying her property with a sense of deep satisfaction. *Her* property. For the first time she felt a real pride of ownership. Though it would be folly to be too optimistic on the basis of just a few good nights' takings, it was a start.

The long wooden jetty was crowded with boats, and under the cheerful green and white awning she could see plenty of people enjoying the fresh seafood lunch in the quayside buffet. Two small power-boats were droning in wide circles out on the lagoon, one towing a water-skier, the other a parascender floating beneath a bright scarlet and gold canopy. Half a dozen windsurfers were scudding in the breeze, while in the rock pools on the southern end of the bay a group of noisy teenagers were scampering around trying to catch the tiny bright coral fish.

Lauren stretched luxuriously. Her slim golden-brown body in the brief yellow bikini attracted many admiring or envious glances, but no one disturbed her peace. She had a way of putting up a 'Keep Off' sign when she wanted to be left alone that was invisible but always effective.

It was her secretary, Maxine, who interrupted her. 'I'm sorry, Miz Henderson,' she said in her babbling-soft local accent, 'there's three ... er ... gentlemen here to see you. They said it was urgent.'

Lauren sat up quickly, shading her face with her hand, and found herself being surveyed by three pairs of eyes. The middle pair were gimlet-small and close together, with all the humanity of a snake. The other two pairs belonged to two great ugly stoats who were looking at her as if she was their next meal. Instinctively she reached for her linen sun-dress and pulled it round her shoulders, buttoning it swiftly, wishing she had been more fully dressed. The stoats were looking at her as if they could still see every curve of her body through the creamy linen, and that made her feel at a distinct disadvantage.

Fear curled in her stomach, but with her usual composure she stepped forward and extended her hand politely. 'Good afternoon, gentlemen,' she said demurely, 'shall we go up to my office?'

The Snake shook her hand briefly. 'Yes, ma'am. Let's be private to discuss our ... business.' The accent ... what? Chicago?

The two stoats just stood and stared at her like kids at a cookie jar, and she felt a surge of anger. Casting them an arctic glance, she turned and led the way into the hotel and up the stairs to her small comfortable office overlooking the casino.

'Well, ma'am, this is a real nice place you've got here,' remarked one of the stoats. He sounded as if he couldn't wait to start ripping it apart, and Lauren had to suppress a quake of fear. Were these the people Alec McGuiness had warned her about? How much did she owe them?

It took every ounce of her self-control to seat herself

calmly behind her desk and say, 'Now, gentlemen, how can I help you?' Even as she spoke she noticed how they moved automatically into position, First Stoat with his back to the door so that no one could get in, Second Stoat covering the window behind her.

Snake took the chair opposite her, and smiled thinly. 'Well now, Mrs Henderson, I'll come straight to the point,' he said. He spread his fingers out on the desk, as if to indicate honesty. 'It's a little matter of a few hundred thousand dollars owing to Mr Straker.'

'Mr Straker?' repeated Lauren, trying rather numbly to remember who Mr Straker was.

'That's right, ma'am. Mr Straker of Straker Investments, Chicago, Illinois. You see, your husband—your *late* husband,' he corrected with spurious sympathy, 'he borrowed some money from Mr Straker a few years ago. A quarter of a million dollars, to be precise.' Lauren nodded, remembering. 'Ah, good. Well, ma'am, you see, the trouble is, your late husband wasn't ... how shall I say it? ... altogether reliable with his payments. In fact, he'd slipped behind rather badly. And now Mr Straker would like his money back.'

Lauren could almost feel the fangs sink into her neck. She summoned her most confident smile. 'Please assure Mr Straker that he will get his money back,' she said calmly. 'As you are aware, things have changed here. I am in sole control of the Blue Lagoon now, and I am confident that I will be able to turn a handsome profit. There will be no further question of falling behind with repayments.'

The Snake's thin lips twisted into a mockery of a smile. 'Perhaps I didn't quite make myself plain, Mrs Henderson,' he said poisonously. 'Mr Straker would like his money now. All of it.'

Lauren feigned astonishment. 'Oh, come now, Mr
... er ...? Look around you. This is an excellent
investment by any standards. Mr Straker can be sure
that his money is secure.'

'I'm afraid Mr Straker don't share your confidence,'
he answered, shaking his head apologetically. 'You
see, it ain't that he's narrow-minded in any way, but
he just don't think a woman on her own is going to be
able to run a joint like this.'

'I'm not lacking in experience, you know,' said
Lauren, beginning to feel desperation. 'While my
husband was alive he took little interest in managing
the place, and virtually left it all to me.'

'I appreciate that, Mrs Henderson,' responded the
Snake, his voice all sweet reasonableness, 'but now he's
dead, you're all on your own.' Suddenly Lauren
became aware that the Second Stoat had moved up
very close behind her, and his hands were on the back
of her chair, holding it still. 'This can be a very
dangerous business for a woman on her own,' went on
the snake, almost purring, 'very dangerous.'

'Oh yes, *very* dangerous,' added Second Stoat, and
his hands closed over her shoulders, pinning her back
against the seat.

'It would be such a pity if anything ... unpleasant
were to happen to such a fine lady as yourself,' the
snake mused.

'Such a pretty lady,' added Second Stoat fondly.
The first stoat had moved in closer, and his eyes were
devouring her hungrily. Lauren would have dearly
loved to scream, but she sensed that to show fear
would be fatal.

'But I'm not entirely alone,' she countered, trying
hard to control the desperation in her voice. At once
she sensed a drawing back. 'I have friends,' she went

on, suddenly feeling safer, 'good friends.' She let her tone imply things unsaid. She knew she had disconcerted them by her unexpected response.

'Well now, lady,' said Snake, his voice as treacherous as thin ice, 'that's real interesting. Mr Straker's gonna be real pleased to hear that.' His eyes were boring into hers like stilettoes of steel. 'And who shall we tell Mr Straker is . . . er . . . looking out for your interests?'

Lauren returned his look steadily. 'Oh, come now,' she said calmly, 'you surely don't expect me to tell you that?'

His eyes glinted with suspicion. 'Mr Straker don't like dealing with people he don't know.' Lauren shrugged her slender shoulders in cool indifference. 'I think we'd better go back and tell Mr Straker what you said. I don't think he's gonna like it,' he added with a sadistic smile.

Lauren gave him her most saccharine smile. 'Perhaps Mr Straker would like to come over to St Arnoux to see his investment for himself?' she suggested with reckless confidence.

'Mr Straker don't like travelling,' said Snake. Mr Straker didn't seem to like much at all, Lauren reflected dryly.

'What a pity. Well, it was nice to have met you, Mr . . . er . . .'

'I didn't give my name,' he replied sharply. 'Goodbye, Mrs Henderson. You'll be hearing from me again.'

He stood up, and with practised timing First Stoat opened the door for him to walk through. Second Stoat leered at her as he passed, and then they were gone, and Lauren was staring at the blank door, shaking from head to foot. Out of the dark swirl in her mind, one thought surfaced. It had been her mention

of 'friends' that had been significant. If she could
convince them that she had powerful protection, would
they leave her alone—long enough to prove that she
could make a profit? She needed time.

Inevitably her thoughts turned to Joe. She didn't
know how far he was involved in the shady world of
smuggling and protection rackets, but the old adage
'better the devil you know' had a lot to recommend it.

A daring plan began to form in her brain. It was not
without risk. If Joe should guess what she was up to,
he would be furious. But she could think of no other
way. She was in a mangrove swamp, and treacherous
roots waited to snare her ankles at every turn.

By Monday the forthcoming card game had become
a magnet for the sensation-hungry jet-setters who
frequented the islands. The marina at the Blue Lagoon
was full, and reports from Hurricane Bay told the
same story. Yachts had even anchored at the tiny
settlement on the north side of the island and the
people were hiring guides to lead them down through
the mangrove forest.

There was almost a carnival atmosphere, and
Lauren's profits were soaring. She dressed with care
for the evening; black, of course. Her dress was of the
finest silk jersey, with a dull sheen that shimmered as
she walked. It was daringly backless, with a neckline
that plunged in a deep V at the front, revealing most
of the soft valley between her breasts. If that didn't
take Joe Daley's mind off his cards, nothing would,
she thought fiercely as she studied her reflection in the
mirror. She had coiled her hair into an elegant fall
over one shoulder, and she wore no jewellery at all
except for the one earring that was to be her stake
tonight.

As she trod gracefully down the stairs to the crowded foyer a flattering murmur of approval ran around the assembled throng. Lauren smiled, and accepted the arm of one of her best customers, whose invitation to drive her over to the other side of the island she had accepted. All the ponies and traps from her stables had been hired, and many more people were planning to walk over. It was a pity that the casino would be almost depleted of customers for a couple of hours, but Lauren knew that after the Canasta game was over many of those going over to Hurricane Bay to watch would return to the Blue Lagoon to gamble away what they had won in side-bets or try to recoup their losses. The odds were running at seven to four in favour of Joe.

It was a lively cavalcade that wound its way along the rough twisting path to Hurricane Bay. The patient ponies clopped their way steadily along the familiar route up over the shoulder of the volcano, skirting above the secret cove that lay hidden in the dark tangle of forest.

Cresting the highest point of the path, they could see the lights of Hurricane Bay spread below them, and hear the surf that on this side of the island could be quite fierce even on the mildest day. Lauren gazed down at the rugged scene, so different from the tranquillity of the Blue Lagoon. The black volcanic rocks here tumbled straight into the sea, with none of the gently-sloping beaches of the leeward side of the island. Unprotected from the blast of the Atlantic gales, the trees had a gaunt twistedness, and there were few of the exotic flowers that lent such bright beauty to her own property.

This place was hard and ruthless, like Joe Daley himself. And yet that very harshness protected the

boats bobbing at anchor in the sheltered water.
Because the volcano had thrown a possessive arm
across the bay, so that although the entrance could be
difficult to navigate, once inside there was safety from
the fierce ocean raging beyond the bar.

There was little scope here for water sports, except
deep-sea fishing; some magnificent shark had been
brought in to be measured and weighed at the wooden
quayside. There was a board to record all the best
catches—Joe's name was among those painted on it.

But the main attraction was gambling. The casino
was open twenty-four hours a day, and the baccarat
bank was reputed to be one of the highest in the
world. The other big attraction was the midnight
cabaret, which regularly boasted big international
stars.

Lauren had often visited Hurricane Bay in the old
days, but never since Joe had taken it over. And oddly
enough, though her late husband had often meandered
off on trips to other casinos around the chain of
islands, he had never visited his next-door neighbour.
People said he was afraid of Joe . . .

Funny that she should suddenly remember Bill. He
had been dead for little more than a week, but already
his existence was all but forgotten by his widow, and
by all the shallow 'friends' with whom he had
surrounded himself.

The lively procession of pony-traps drew up in
front of the forbidding fastness of the Hurricane Bay
Hotel. Joe came down the steps to meet them,
devastatingly attractive in his customary white dinner-
jacket, acknowledging the greetings of the crowd with
a wave of his hand.

He helped Lauren down from her trap, greeting her
with formal politeness, but his eyes gleamed devilishly

as they swept down over her body in open appreciation. 'I see you've decided to give yourself an unfair advantage,' he drawled with amusement.

'What *can* you mean?' she returned, her lashes fluttering flirtatiously.

His eyes lingered over the warm curve of her breasts. 'The scenery, I assure you, is breathtaking,' he murmured huskily.

Lauren's heart was racing, her breathing unsteady. His gaze was stirring the embers of a response that she would have preferred to believe had died. She was beginning to regret that she had chosen this subtle display of her charms. She found it hard to ignore the way her body shimmered with excitement when he looked at her in that particular way. She fought to control the tumultuous rise and fall of her breasts.

'You're very flattering,' she said a little unsteadily.

He drew her hand possessively through his arm, and led her into his lair. The fortress had been built by men of the British Navy at one of the high points of its history, and everywhere solid British oak was much in evidence, along with gleaming brass. The impression of being aboard one of Nelson's frigates was begun by the well-preserved ship's cannon in the lofty entrance hall, trained dauntingly at guests entering the wide front doors, and the theme was continued unobtrusively throughout the hotel.

To the left was a luxurious restaurant, where a French chef had built himself a twenty-year reputation for his mouthwatering ways of serving locally-caught fish, that attracted gourmets from all over the world. On the other side was the lively nightclub, where couples were dancing to the music of a very good resident band.

'Would you like a drink first?' asked Joe, 'or would you prefer to go straight upstairs?'

Lauren glanced around at the eager gamblers pressing in behind them. 'I understand there's a lot of money riding on this game,' she said with a smile. 'Perhaps we'd better not keep them waiting.'

'Okay, sweetheart. Let's give the punters what they want,' he drawled.

The gaming-room was reached by a sweeping flight of stairs that split in two at a half-landing and curved round to meet before a pair of wide, strapped-oak doors. On the upper floors was accommodation for a hundred guests in well-appointed suites, and above that comfortable staff accommodation and Joe's own luxurious flat.

There was a hushed intensity in the atmosphere that was barely lightened by the stir of interest as they entered the gaming room. A table had been set aside for them in a cleared space, to allow plenty of room for the crowd that was gathering to watch them. A glass of Lauren's favourite sparkling mineral water was set at her elbow, and Joe had his usual heavy crystal tumbler of rye whisky.

'I see you've brought your stake,' remarked Joe as they took their seats.

'Of course,' she responded lightly.

'One earring—very rakish. You're very confident,' he teased.

She slanted him a flirtatious glance under her lashes. 'You may have won once, but that doesn't mean you're going to win every time,' she purred, deliberately seductive.

'Doesn't it?' His eyes told her that he was attuned to the hidden levels of the conversation. Though they were surrounded by people, Lauren felt as if they were alone, fighting out their secret battle of wills.

Joe handed her the two packs of cards to split the seals, and she handed them back to him to shuffle for the first cut. They were not gambling for points this time, only to win, so the game was fast and exhilarating, both fiercer and more lighthearted than the first. There was a good deal of humorous banter between the players and the spectators. Unhampered as she was by the fear of losing money she couldn't afford, Lauren's game was a match for Joe's, and though he gave her no quarter she won by a narrow margin of just two hundred points. There was a ripple of applause, and general agreement that it had been one of the best games of Canasta seen on the islands in a long time.

Joe joined warmly in the applause. 'Well done,' he congratulated her. 'That was brilliantly played. I never suspected you were holding queens.'

Lauren smiled with glowing triumph. 'My winnings, if you please?' she asked coquettishly, holding out her hand.

'Ah yes.' He took the earring from his pocket and dropped it into her palm.

'Thank you.' Her face was serene as she clipped the gem to her small earlobe, but her brain was in overdrive, studying his eyes. Did he know that it was a fake? He gave her no clue. 'I warned you that I would win this time,' she teased.

'Ah, but I won the pleasure of your company for the evening,' he responded smoothly. 'I feel that's worth a few diamonds.'

'How gallant you're becoming,' she remarked.

'Not bad for trash, eh?'

She tensed at his unexpected invocation of a half-forgotten memory—an echo of a long-ago conversation. Was he deliberately seeking to undermine her

composure? 'You're ageing well after all,' she
countered sweetly. 'It must be the infusion of money.'

'No doubt,' he responded in sardonic amusement.
'Shall we go downstairs?' He rose to his feet, and
offered her his arm to escort her downstairs to the
nightclub.

As they entered, the singer with the group glanced
towards them with a gleaming grin, and promptly
launched into an impromptu calypso celebrating
Lauren's win. As usual with calypso, the lyrics were
obliquely suggestive, and comprehensible only to
those who understood the local slang. But everyone
could guess at the meaning, and laughed and
applauded happily.

Lauren felt slightly uncomfortable standing in the
doorway, so close to Joe, the focus of all eyes. She
knew that assumptions were being made about the
nature of their relationship which would make her
strategy all the more dangerous. As Joe led her to a
table reserved for him at the edge of the semi-circular
dance-floor she was aware of an air of possessiveness
about him that made her want to run away as fast as
she could. But she had to stay, and play out her secret
game. It was the only way she could think of to save
the Blue Lagoon.

A magnum of champagne nestled in a silver bucket
beside the table, and Joe opened it and offered her a
sparkling glass.

'To your victory,' he toasted her, his eyes smiling,
but she was aware that he was watching her closely.
She inclined her head in acknowledgement of the
salute, and sipped her champagne, letting her gaze
rove interestedly around the Great Hall of the
fortress. No expense had been spared to transform it
into a luxurious nightclub. A timbered gallery ran

around three sides, offering excellent views of the stage, and impressive brass chandeliers swung from the ceiling, lending a baronial splendour to the setting.

'Would you like to dance?' Lauren's eyes flickered swiftly to Joe's face, a sudden surge of nervous tension contracting her heart. Without waiting for her to reply he took her hand and drew her to her feet.

The dance floor was crowded, and he had to hold her close in the circle of his arms. His breath fanned her cheek, and as she rested her hands lightly against his shoulders she could sense the vibrant power of the muscles beneath the smooth cloth of his jacket. She was aware of everything about him—the way his hair curled crisply over the nape of his neck, the slight roughness of his cheek. He was a good dancer, moving lightly to the music, moulding her body to his so that they were one entity, driven by the subtle, compelling rhythms of the band.

The music ended, breaking the spell, and Joe took her back to their table. As the floor cleared, spotlights of emerald, sapphire and amethyst swirled through the darkness, and from a door at the back of the small stage a fair-haired young man in a very sharp suit bounced out, a microphone in his hand.

Lauren sat sipping her champagne, her mind numb. Dancing in Joe's arms had given her a warning of what she would have to face if she went ahead with her plans. Held so close against that hard, masculine body, she had been aware of a thrill of response that she knew was going to become increasingly difficult to control.

But she allowed no sign of her inner turmoil to betray her. She laughed at the comedian's rather risqué jokes without hearing them, all too aware of

Joe's dark gaze resting on her, warming her flesh as if he were caressing her.

The next act was a singer, a smoky-voiced blonde, and she was very good, playing up to the predominantly male audience with her feline walk and sultry smile. Lauren didn't miss the smouldering light in her eyes as she looked at Joe, nor the responsive gleam in his. Was this his current mistress? As she watched the secret byplay between them she became convinced of it. The glance the singer slanted at her was pure acid. She felt an illogical glow of satisfaction. So the girl was jealous? She'd have even greater cause before the night was over!

When the girl finished her two songs, Lauren applauded, and remarked warmly to Joe on her talent. 'Of course,' he responded with an enigmatic smile. 'I always have the best that money can buy.'

'You're fortunate that you can afford it,' she responded with a touch of asperity.

'Money has its advantages,' he countered ironically. 'But then you know that, don't you, sweetheart? None better.'

'I wouldn't sell my soul for it,' she retorted with dignity.

His insolent gaze assessed her as if she were ripe fruit on display in the market. 'Ah, but then it isn't your soul I want,' he reminded her, his voice soft and evil.

Lauren felt her cheeks flush a heated scarlet. 'You make it sound no better than hustling on the waterfront in Port-of-Spain!' she hissed angrily.

His dark eyes captured hers before she could defend herself. 'Oh, it will be better,' he murmured, 'I can assure you of that.'

Around her she could hear laughter, and was dimly

aware that the sharp young man was on stage again, telling jokes. But she was alone with Joe, and her body was remembering.

A cool soft voice behind her said, 'You didn't tell me you were having a guest tonight, Joe.'

Lauren glanced up into a pair of eyes as green as a cat's. Joe's hard mouth curved into a sardonic smile. 'Clancy! Meet Lauren,' he drawled in a voice that Lauren didn't like. The two women exchanged brief glances that took in every detail. The singer was reed-thin, with a feline sexiness that seemed to exude from every pore.

With a discreet gesture, Joe told one of the waiters to bring another chair. He patted Clancy intimately on her sleekly-moulded derriere. 'Sit down, sweetheart,' he invited.

Lauren felt a stab of anger, hearing him address the other girl with that casual endearment. Clancy leaned very close to Joe, turning up to him the full megawatt power of those dazzling green eyes.

'Could I have some champagne, Joe?' she pouted.

'It's Lauren's champagne,' Joe told her provocatively. 'She just beat me at cards.'

'So I heard.' Clancy shafted a venomous glance at Lauren. 'You run the other casino, don't you?' she asked.

'That's right,' Lauren responded, feeling like a mongoose watching a snake.

'I've heard a lot about you.' Her tone implied that none of it was good. Lauren merely lifted one eyebrow a fraction of an inch. 'I suppose you two must have known each other a long time,' Clancy went on edgily.

'A *very* long time,' Lauren confirmed with a smile that was intended to convey a thousand other messages.

Joe leaned back in his seat, his eyes sliding from one to the other in cynical enjoyment of the situation. Lauren's palm itched to hit him.

'Lauren liked your act,' he told Clancy with the air of one deliberately stirring troubled waters.

Clancy batted her furry eyelashes at him. 'But did *you* like it, darling?' she purred.

'As always. You're a great little performer,' he smiled, his voice caressing her. She shafted a smug little smile at Lauren. 'I'll really miss you when you've gone.' Green eyes and black turned swiftly to his face. 'I'd love to extend your contract,' he went on, a heavy note of intimacy in his voice, 'but I had someone else lined up a long time ago to fill the slot.'

Lauren's stared at him dazedly. He was deliberately choosing his words to add a subtle implication to them. Her teeth bit into the trembling inner softness of her lip as she realised that her instinctive reaction was one of pleasure. Just as if she was still in love with him.

Clancy looked towards her with open hostility. 'I didn't realise you were planning to replace me,' she grated angrily to Joe. 'I thought you were completely satisfied.'

'Oh, I have been,' he assured her silkily, 'but you knew from the beginning that it was only a short-term arrangement.'

The girl blinked sharply, her mouth tight. 'I see. Well, if you'll excuse me, I'd better go and phone my agent.'

'It's after midnight,' Joe reminded her gently.

'So? I'll get him out of bed. It's about time he started earning his ten per cent!'

She stalked away, her head held high. Lauren watched her go, her own emotions in turmoil. Taking refuge in anger, she turned on Joe in fury for his cynical cruelty. 'That wasn't very nice,' she remarked acidly.

Joe shrugged his wide shoulders indifferently. 'Clancy can look after herself,' he said coolly, 'she's a professional.'

'Do you always terminate your—er—contracts so ruthlessly?' she asked dryly. One dark eyebrow lifted fractionally. 'She was your mistress as well, wasn't she?' she challenged hotly.

His eyes glinted satanically. 'What do you expect?' he responded obliquely.

Lauren warned herself to be careful. Once before she had thought he was making it easy for her to weave her schemes, and had found instead that he was the spider and she the fly. She answered in a low voice, 'And yet you're asking me to marry you, Joe? You couldn't expect me to tolerate your mistresses on the premises.'

He flashed such a searching look at her that she could not meet his eyes. 'Do I detect some wavering in your determined refusal?' he enquired a little sharply.

'I just felt . . . we shouldn't rush into anything,' she responded demurely, her eyes lowered.

He leaned towards her, capturing her hand, and his voice was very low. 'If you don't know your own mind by now, Lauren . . .'

She drew back, her heart pounding like thunder, and swept him a carefully rehearsed glance. 'Perhaps . . . if we were to get engaged . . .?'

She held her breath. Would he start asking awkward questions, or would his pride lead him to believe that he had succeeded in making her jealous of the singer? There was still a trace of suspicion in his eyes as he sat back in his seat, but his laugh was sardonic. 'Now why do I get the feeling that you're up to something?' he asked with dry amusement.

Lauren felt a little surge of panic, but kept it from her voice as she asked, 'Why on earth should you think that?'

'I don't know.' Abruptly he sat forward again, drawing her hand into both of his, compelling her to look into his eyes. 'Be careful, Lauren,' he warned in a voice that was low but unmistakably menacing. 'Don't play with fire.' She caught her breath, suddenly afraid that she was revealing far too much. But he let her go, and sat back again, smiling that devastating smile, his eyes guarded. 'Okay, sweetheart, we'll get engaged,' he conceded with tolerant amusement. 'Ah—is this to be a secret engagement, or do we make a public announcement?'

Lauren began to allow herself to relax a little. 'Oh, there's no need to keep it from our friends,' she said lightly, 'though I don't think we need to tell the whole world.'

He nodded, his eyes watching her every reaction. 'And is it to be a long engagement?' he went on.

She shrugged her shoulders with studied non-chalance. 'I hadn't given it much thought,' she lied smoothly. 'There's no rush, is there?'

'If you say so,' he agreed, his expression unreadable. His hand closed over hers again. 'Now that you've agreed to be my wife I don't think you'll go back on your word.' There was an unmistakable thread of steel in his voice, and Lauren felt herself quiver with apprehension. Joe held a power over her still, a power which part of her did not even want to resist. If only he really cared about her, if only she could surrender herself into his arms and let him protect her from the storms that were raging around her, from the evil men who were threatening her.

But what was the use of 'if only'? Her mind cleared,

and she focused her eyes on that hard, satanic face against the backdrop of the smoke-filled nightclub. This was the reality, she warned herself. She was fencing with a ruthless opponent, and she must never drop her guard, not even for a moment.

He still held her hand, and his thumb was gently stroking her wrist. She wished he wouldn't do it, but there was no way she could stop him. The sensation was spreading up her arm like a warm glow, undermining her ability to concentrate on the moves she had to make. It took all her will-power to draw back.

'It's getting rather late,' she said, her voice quavering a little. 'I'd better be going.' She essayed a light laugh. 'I have a nightclub to run too, you know.'

'You're leaving?'

'Yes, I . . .' Her voice trailed away under the look in his eyes. Suddenly her whole body was aflame.

'Why don't you stay?' he coaxed, his voice rasping-soft, touching chords deep inside her, beyond the reach of the rational part of her mind.

'No, I . . . I can't, I . . .'

'You weren't so unwilling once.'

Lauren flushed scarlet. In all the years that had passed, the events of that fateful summer when she was seventeen had never been so directly alluded to by either of them. A veil had been drawn across it, and it was painful to rip it aside. Her hand trembled in his. 'That was a long time ago,' she whispered with difficulty. She was close to throwing away her whole game-plan. She forced herself to smile, though it quivered on her lips. 'I was just a silly, naïve little kid. I've learnt a lot since then.' Her voice and smile became more confident as she added, 'I think I'd rather wait until I've got your ring on my finger.'

Joe sat back, laughing softly. 'Okay, sweetheart. If

that's the way you want to play it,' he drawled, his words underlined with unmistakable mockery. 'But this sure ain't gonna be a long engagement!' He picked up the champagne and poured her another sparkling glass. He lifted his own glass to his lips in sardonic salute. 'To our future happiness,' he toasted her ironically, his eyes lingering over the slender curves of her body with a possessiveness that made her quiver as if he were touching her. 'We'll sail up to St V tomorrow,' he went on. 'I think it will be expected that I buy you the biggest diamond in the West Indies.'

'Not by me,' protested Lauren in genuine surprise.

He lifted a quizzical eyebrow. 'No? You intrigue me. Can I hope that you're not marrying me for my money after all?'

Lauren laughed uneasily. 'Don't be silly, Joe,' she demurred. 'Why should I need to do that?'

'Don't you?' he challenged. His eyes probed hers, dangerously perceptive.

But her defences were safely intact again, and she allowed a slight tantalising smile to play around her lips. 'Of course not, Joe. I do hope I haven't given that impression?'

'Not at all. Though I confess the reason isn't entirely clear.'

'You're too modest, Joe,' she purred.

He laughed harshly. 'That has never been one of my failings,' he remarked. 'Okay, sweetheart, if you're determined to be chaste, I'll concede defeat—at least for tonight. Come on, I'll take you home.'

'That really isn't necessary . . .'

'Of course it is,' he insisted. 'Surely you won't deny me an innocent good night kiss on your doorstep?' He threw up his hand in a gesture of self-mockery. 'A good night kiss! This will ruin my reputation!'

Lauren gurgled with laughter. 'A little patience will do you good,' she advised him boldly. Her confidence was returning. She had got over the first hurdle more easily than she had dared hope.

But in spite of the lighthearted banter, as they drove home through the cool moonlight Lauren felt again that chill of apprehension. She studied Joe's hard profile as he concentrated on the task of keeping the wheels of the pony-trap safely on the rough road. His warning that she was playing with fire had been quite unnecessary. How long could she keep him at bay, holding out the promise that she would marry him, while resisting his expert seduction?

He had already hinted that he was not going to agree to a long engagement. His reaction had been exactly what she had feared. Joe Daley was not a patient man. But every precious week she could win would improve her chance of keeping the Blue Lagoon. If her phoney engagement to Joe persuaded Mr Straker to leave her alone, if she could show a profit . . . And once they had accepted her, she would find a way to end the engagement, turning Joe's pride against him so that he would leave her alone for ever.

It was a strategy conceived in desperation, and it would take every ounce of her wit and determination to win. The dreams that she had once dreamed had returned to haunt her as nightmares. Once she had thought that to be Joe's wife would be heaven on earth. But she was a long way from heaven now. She was holding a time-bomb that could blow up in her face at any moment. She had only to glance at Joe's face to realise that the fuse was dangerously short. Time. She must have time . . .

He drew the pony to a halt beside the Blue Lagoon Hotel, and turned to her, his face shadowy in the moonlight. 'Well, sweetheart,' he drawled mockingly, 'do I get my good night kiss, or do I have to wait for that too?'

'I have to put the pony away,' she countered defensively.

Joe whistled, and a moment later Scoot, the stable-lad, appeared. He had looked after the ponies since he was a boy, in the days when Joe had been manager of the Blue Lagoon, and his eyes lit with joy when he saw him. 'Hey, boss!' he cried in obvious delight. 'How you doin', man?'

Joe jumped down from the trap and slapped hands with the younger man in the exuberant island manner. 'Not so bad, Scoot. Yourself?'

'I got myself hitched up, man. Whoo-wee! Ain't it wonderful?'

'Congratulations, Scoot. And you can congratulate me. I'm going to marry Mrs Henderson.'

Scoot whistled. 'Really? You ain't puttin' me on? Well, sure, congratulations, boss,' he beamed. 'Congratulations, Mrs Henderson.'

'Thank you, Scoot,' murmured Lauren as Joe helped her down from the trap. It had shaken her a little to hear the words spoken so casually. Foolishly, she hadn't thought of ordinary people—her staff, the regular cruising clientele—knowing of her engagement and discussing it with genuine good-will. She had thought only of the scandalmongers, whom she would enjoy setting in a spin, and of Mr Straker and his sort.

'You gonna take over here again, boss?' Scoot wanted to know.

'Nothing's been decided yet, Scoot,' said Joe, draping his arm casually over the stable-boy's

shoulders and walking along with him as he led the
pony back to the stalls. 'But you know that whatever
happens . . .'

Their voices faded as they turned the corner.
Lauren leaned weakly against the trap. Joe had spoken
with such calm certainty. 'I'm going to marry Mrs
Henderson.' He wanted her, and now that he almost
had her within his grasp he wouldn't easily let her go.
She closed her eyes, the image of his strongly-carved
features etched into her mind so vividly that she could
see him as if he were standing beside her now. She saw
him smiling down at her, his eyes warm as they had
been once, long ago.

She had loved him then as only the young and
innocent can love, without reservation. The echoes of
that love still called to her down the years, tugging at
her heart as if it had never died under the crushing
brutality of Joe's rejection. She could feel it now, a
disturbing eddy swirling in her pulse, quickening her
heartbeat . . .

'Shall we walk for a while?'

Lauren opened startled eyes. She had not heard him
return, and before she could escape he had his arm
around her and was luring her unwilling footsteps
down the moonlit path towards the secret darkness on
the southern side of the bay, where the whispering
palms offered a veil of seclusion to lovers.

Her sensitised antennae had picked up a subtle
change in his manner that she couldn't quite define.
What had he and Scoot talked about during that brief
spell when they were out of earshot? Was he using her
own staff to spy on her? She fought to control the
anger and suspicion that raged inside her. She
couldn't afford to let emotion get the better of her.
She *had* to remain in control.

It was far from easy, strolling through the shadowy garden with Joe. The night sky was a velvet blue-black cloak, drifted with a million diamonds. The air was rich with the sweet perfume of frangipani, alive with the song of cicadas. The moonlight lay like silver on the smooth surface of the lagoon.

Held close in the circle of Joe's strong arm, Lauren felt the seductive lure of the romantic atmosphere. It would be so easy to succumb, to let Joe win the fight. If she surrendered, surely he would not be cruel in his victory? And yet she had made that mistake before, only to have him take everything she offered and then just walk away. She couldn't take that again.

He led her down to a quiet corner of the garden, where the night hid them from prying eyes, and then he turned her into his arms. This was the moment she had dreaded. He was going to kiss her, and she wasn't ready—she would never be ready. She didn't want to look up into his eyes, and focused instead on the top button of his shirt. He had taken off his bow-tie and unfastened his collar, and at the base of his throat clustered fine dark curls . . .

'So, Lauren,' he said softly, 'are you going to tell me what you're playing at?'

'I don't know what you mean,' she protested in a half-strangled whisper.

'Oh yes, you do. Don't play games with me, Lauren. You should know better than that after all these years. You won't win.'

'Don't be so sure,' she returned defiantly, lifting her eyes to his in reckless challenge. It was a mistake. His dark gaze held her, hypnotising her, and she was powerless to resist when his mouth lowered to claim hers.

Firmly, insistently, he coaxed apart her lips, seeking

all the secret, sensitive places, igniting fires of response in her until the steel in her spine melted in the heat he was generating, and she curved into his powerful embrace, allowing him to mould her body tightly to his.

He was making her forcibly aware of the savage male hunger that he was going to expect her to satisfy, sooner or later, and she quivered with a soft feminine submissiveness that it was almost impossible to control. Deep inside her body memories stirred, and clamoured to be re-lived. She was surrendering without thought or resistance to a tidal wave of desire that was sweeping her away.

Joe's teeth and tongue were doing crazy things to the lobe of her ear, and his kisses warmed the long sensitive curve of her neck until she shivered from the heat. Her arms had crept around his neck of their own volition, her fingers curled in the crisp hair at the nape of his neck. His hands stroked down the length of her bare back with slow, warm sensuality, and she felt the slow burn of passion rising inside her. His fingers slid inside her dress to caress her naked breast with a secret intimacy that brought a moan of intense pleasure to her lips.

She clung to his strength, knowing that he was mastering her with an ease that proved he was right. She couldn't win. He only had to touch her to claim her. All her cool self-possession had crumbled before him. She was his, she always had been, she always would be. She didn't stand a chance.

And then abruptly he let her go. She swayed dizzily, reaching for him, sobbing his name in desperate pleading. He drew away from her, his laughter mocking. 'I warned you,' he reminded her harshly. 'Let's have no more nonsense about getting engaged.

Tomorrow we go to St Vincent and make the arrangements for the wedding. You marry me by the end of the month, or not at all.'

He turned on his heel, and vanished into the night.

Lauren stood for a long time in the darkness, fighting to retrieve the scattered threads of her composure. Her breathing was ragged, her eyes stinging with tears. She must have been crazy to think that she could outplay Joe! He had wanted her for a long time, and she had kept him waiting. Now he was going to make her pay, if he could. She had seen it in his eyes as they walked down through the garden, a glittering anger behind the hot embers of desire. He knew that, though she had consented to marry him, she eluded him still, and he was determined to have her on his own terms.

She felt shamed by the memory of how completely she had responded to his kiss. Her body was still shimmering with the heat of his touch. It had been one thing to plan this phoney engagement in the safe solitude of her office, but to play out the game, to allow Joe the intimacy her promise gave him the right to expect, was another matter. How would she find the will-power to resist him if tonight, the first time for seven years that he had kissed her, she had melted in his arms as if she was still in love with him?

The end of the month. Two weeks. Would it be enough time? She had hoped for longer—a couple of months. It wasn't very seemly to be rushing into another marriage so soon after her husband's death. But Joe wouldn't consider that, of course. He wouldn't consider anything but what *he* wanted. He was like a hurricane, battering to the ground everything that stood in his path.

Two weeks: it had to be enough. And then she

would call off her wedding to Joe at the very last minute. With luck, he would be so angry that he would sell Hurricane Bay and leave the island, and she would never see him again. Once the Blue Lagoon was safe, it wouldn't matter. Slowly she walked back towards the brightly-lit casino.

CHAPTER FIVE

'Mrs Henderson?'

'Yes, Raoul, what is it?' The grave face of her head croupier brought Lauren's mind swiftly back to more immediate problems. Raoul was worried.

'Trouble, Mrs Henderson.' His eyes flickered towards the baccarat table. To the right of the dealer sat a thin, balding man, calmly studying his cards. He was not in any way striking, except for the sharpness of his grey eyes.

'He's been at the table since ten o'clock, and he's winning heavily,' Raoul told her quietly. 'The backers are all following him now, too.'

'How much are we down?' The figure made Lauren whistle. 'Is he cheating?'

'He must be, but I can't see how. I've been watching him for over four hours—I've even taken the deal myself. But he's beating the bank at least seventy per cent of the time.'

'That's way over the odds,' muttered Lauren fiercely. 'Damn! Just when we don't need it, we have to attract a shark.' She cast her eyes around the room. It was still fairly quiet; some of those who had returned early from Hurricane Bay were gathered around the roulette wheel or the blackjack table, but about a dozen non-playing backers were leaning over the baccarat game that was in progress, and the excitement of big money changing hands crackled in the air like lightning.

Lauren moved over silently to watch. It was a

measure of the intensity of the game that few acknowledged her presence. Alain, the baccarat dealer, was one of the most experienced croupiers in the islands, and a betraying knot of tension above his temple suggested to Lauren that he was not involved in the treachery.

She watched the thin man place his stake. Five hundred dollars. The other bets were quickly placed until the bank was covered, and Lauren could see at once that very little money had been staked on the left-hand side of the table. The cards were dealt—two in turn to the two principal players, and two to the dealer himself. The thin man tipped up his cards, glanced at them almost uninterestedly, then flipped them over. He had a five and a four. 'Natural nine,' he said flatly.

A ripple of approval ran round the table. The other player accepted a card, and received a three. Alain turned his cards over—he had a nine and a seven. '*Six à la banc*,' he announced. The left-hand side had scored only five, so lost their stakes, but the pay-out to the right was huge.

Again and again Lauren watched as the sequence repeated itself. She watched the thin man, she watched Alain, she watched the other punters. Nothing. She moved round unobtrusively to stand behind Alain, and discreetly but carefully studied the cards that had been tossed into the basket. No marks, nothing. If the man was cheating, and she was certain that he was, he was very, very good.

She walked back to stand beside Raoul. 'What's his name?' she asked quietly.

'Evans—Bernard Evans. He's from England.'

'Is he alone?'

'Yes. That is, he arrived alone, and I haven't seen

him talking to anyone in particular,' Raoul told her. 'He's got a smallish cabin cruiser, the *Maid of Kent*. Discreet. He docked earlier this evening, and came straight up to the casino.'

Lauren considered the information carefully. Evans—what a bland name! She had little doubt that his arrival was not a coincidence. But who had set him on to her? Straker, intent on proving that he was right, and forcing her out of business? Or Joe? Would he resort to such underhand tactics to frighten her into accepting his proposal?

Whichever, it was a disaster. Although technically she could refuse admission to anyone she chose, if she barred a winner for no apparent reason but that he was winning she would make herself very unpopular, and in the long run lose as much if not more. No, she had to catch him, or she had to stand by and watch him pocket her profits for as long as she dared. How long—two nights, three? Always this dangerous game, balancing the odds, playing for time. She was so tired of it. Almost it would be better to give in, accept Joe's terms, marry him. She could no longer pretend to herself that she was immune to his physical attraction. If that alone could be enough, marriage to Joe could have a great deal to recommend it.

But she couldn't do it. The steely resolve hardened in her spine again. 'Very well,' she instructed Raoul quietly, 'close the casino at five o'clock sharp. If Mr Evans is still with us tomorrow night, I'll deal myself.'

'Yes, Mrs Henderson.'

Lauren walked slowly back into the half-empty nightclub, and dutifully began her regular round of chatting to customers, making them feel welcome and relaxed. Many of them were 'gambling widows', whose husbands left them alone night after night to find their own entertainment while they congregated round the hushed baize tables next door. Beautiful young women, glittering like tinsel, anxiously watching for every line and wrinkle that would mean they were to be traded in for a younger model. And the not so wealthy young men who battened on them, flattering them and making up to them in return for expensive presents and the chance of being invited to join a free jaunt to the next resort.

The fixed, artificial smile that was the best Lauren could muster in such company was accepted at face value, as was everything else in their shallow lives.

As soon as she could she slipped upstairs to the office, and sat alone in the cool quiet, running over and over in her mind figures and calculations, schemes and plans.

If Straker insisted on having his money back, could she raise finance elsewhere? Who would offer her the best terms? Cold realism forced her to admit that it was unlikely she would be able to borrow when she was so heavily mortgaged already. And interest rates were high. Leaning back in the leather swivel seat, she closed her eyes wearily.

Even in her dreams she could find no respite. She was dealing baccarat, and losing every time, but the Stoat was holding her in her seat, forcing her to deal again and again. She looked up at her opponent, expecting to see the thin ascetic face of Bernard Evans, the card-sharp. Instead, it was Joe, his hard face merciless as he stripped her of all her defences, cruelly offering to write off her losses in return for her submission.

The image was so real that she woke with a gasp, shaking from head to foot. She rose, and walked over to the window that looked down over the casino. The

lights had been turned on—it must have been that
which had woken her—and the croupiers were moving
around, stacking cards, checking chips. Alain and
Raoul were sitting at the empty baccarat table,
meticulously checking every one of the three hundred
and twelve cards used in the game. Lauren went
downstairs and joined them.

'I *know* he was cheating,' groaned Alain miserably.
'What I don't know is how.'

Lauren picked up the cards he had already checked,
and began checking them herself, minutely examining
the backs and the edges for the finest trace of a mark.
There was absolutely nothing. 'There's nothing we
can do,' she sighed. 'We just have to hope he doesn't
stay long enough to milk us dry.'

'He won't stay long,' said Raoul with certainty. 'He
won't risk letting us get to know him, spotting how he
does it. Three or four nights at most, I should say.'

Three or four. Could she stand tonight's losses
again? Grimly she acknowledged that she had no
choice. 'Tomorrow night we watch him like hawks,' she
vowed fiercely. 'I will deal. I'm sorry, Alain,' she added
quickly before the croupier could bridle, 'I'm certainly
not accusing you of anything. But if I'm going to be
fleeced, I might as well be fleeced in person.'

Alain looked relieved. If the Blue Lagoon went
under, he would need another job, and it wouldn't
enhance his reputation to be known as the croupier
who had sunk his casino.

Lauren snapped the cards together impatiently. She
must *not* think so defeatistly. She still had a chance.
Though she held no trumps, and her aces had all been
stolen, if she played with skill she could still win. So
long as she kept her nerve . . .

*   *   *

She slept badly, and woke abruptly to the shrill sound of the telephone ringing beside her bed. She gazed at it, fear knotting her stomach, then she reached out a trembling hand to pick up the receiver.

'Call for you, Miz Henderson,' came Maxine's voice.

Lauren took a deep, steadying breath. 'Thank you, Maxine.' She sat up in bed, trying to compose herself.

'Good morning, Mrs Henderson.' The voice was cold and mocking, the Chicago accent nerve-twistingly familiar. 'Did you sleep well?' The Snake.

'Good afternoon,' she said calmly, flickering a glance at the clock on her bedside table. 'Who is speaking, please?'

'You know me, Mrs Henderson,' came the voice, menacingly venomous. 'How are your profits?'

'Excellent, thank you,' she responded promptly, glad that he could not see how her hand was shaking. 'You can assure Mr Straker that this month's repayment, with full interest, will be made on time.'

'That isn't what Mr Straker wants, Mrs Henderson. He can get better rates of interest than you are paying, and on much shorter term loans. He wants his capital, Mrs Henderson.' The voice was a monotone, the threat underplayed but unmistakable.

Lauren summoned every ounce of her self-control. 'Perhaps I could speak to Mr Straker himself?' she asked steadily.

'Why should you want to do that, Mrs Henderson?' he purred.

'I'd like to discuss that with Mr Straker,' she countered.

'Mr Straker prefers to leave all his business dealings to me,' was his response. 'If you have anything to say . . .?'

'I was wondering . . . if Mr Straker would be

interested in renegotiating the terms of the loan,' she
said as calmly as she could. But as soon as she said it
she knew she'd made a mistake. She could almost see
the Snake's gloating face at the other end of the phone.

'Why don't you go to your influential friends, Mrs
Henderson?' The voice was pure evil. 'I'm sure they'd
be happy to help you out.'

'I . . .'

'I don't think Mr Straker will want to listen to your
proposals, Mrs Henderson,' the voice continued
silkily. 'I'll be visiting you again very soon to discuss
settlement of the debt. In the meantime, my friends
will be around to . . . ah . . . protect Mr Straker's
investment. Goodbye, Mrs Henderson.'

The phone went dead. Lauren stared at it, biting
her lip. They were pressuring her, trying to make her
panic. She had to think. But the phone rang again,
shrilling through her disordered nerves, and she
snatched it up. 'Yes?'

'Hi there, sweetheart.' The New York drawl was
miraculously reassuring, and Lauren couldn't keep the
relief from her voice.

'Oh, Joe, it's you!'

'Sure it's me. We've got business over the water,
remember? If you don't get your beautiful little butt
down here in ten minutes, I'll be up to fetch you.'

His tone was light and teasing, but there was a
thread of steel in his voice that warned her that he
would brook no opposition. Her heart began to flutter
as she remembered the way he had held her last night.
Joe too was pressuring her, refusing to give her time to
think. He would certainly carry out his threat if she
didn't hurry, and if he found her half-dressed . . .!

She would go along with is plans for today. That
would at least give her a little time; even a week would

be better than nothing. If only she could find someone else to lend her the money . . .

She showered swiftly, and scrubbed herself dry. From her wardrobe she pulled a batik-printed wrap-around skirt, and a dainty sun-top of fine Sea Island cotton. Twisting her hair quickly into a neat coil on top of her head, she hurried from the room and ran lightly down the stairs.

Joe was waiting at the bottom, looking cool and rakishly relaxed in cotton slacks and a short-sleeved linen shirt, open at the collar to reveal the clustering of fine dark curls at the base of his throat. Lauren had to avert her eyes in sudden dry-mouthed awareness of the sheer physical impact of his presence, an impact that the years had done nothing to diminish. His powerful frame was as lean and muscular as ever, the animal magnetism as potent.

He took her arm possessively, and she felt the force of his compelling masculinity exuding from him with no apparent effort on his part, and the deep feminine core of her being ached to respond. But she dared not let him see weakness, so she spoke with a tolerable assumption of her usual composure. 'I hope I haven't kept you waiting?'

'Oh, but you have,' he responded promptly, his black eyes gleaming with devilish amusement.

But she wasn't going to get drawn into that one. 'You should have warned me that you intended dragging me out at the crack of dawn,' she uttered with a world-weary sigh.

Joe laughed infectiously. 'It's half past one,' he informed her with mock-severity. 'You're getting into some very decadent habits, young lady. It's time you were taken in hand. I wouldn't mind betting that you haven't even had breakfast.'

'I haven't,' she admitted ruefully as they stepped out into the bright sunshine of early afternoon.

'Never mind. There's some food on the boat.' His boat was a neat thirty-foot motor-cruiser, sleek and powerful. She was called *Midnight Lady*, and Lauren wondered which of his mistresses he'd named her for. She thought of asking, to show that she didn't care, but he interrupted her by saying, 'Who was your call from?'

Suddenly Lauren was wary. 'My call?'

'You had a call on the line when I arrived. From Chicago. Who was it?' He had climbed over the transom on to the boat's teak deck, and turned to help her aboard, his eyes searching her face. She hesitated, her mind suddenly unsure of the wisdom of stepping aboard the boat.

'It was business,' she responded tersely, resisting the insistent tugging of his hand.

'Who was it?' he demanded relentlessly.

'You don't own me yet,' she countered fiercely.

Without warning he dragged her roughly into the boat and into his arms. She fell against him, the breath driven from her body, but he gave her no time to recover, smothering her gasp of protest with a kiss that was savagely insistent, bruising her lips and ravaging her defenceless mouth. Her hands braced instinctively against his shoulders, trying to force him away, but her strength was no match for him and neither was her will. Her resistance moved on shifting sands, crumbled, and fell; her arms folded themselves around his neck, and her body submitted to the hardness of his embrace.

As Joe felt her yield he gentled. His lips moved arousingly over hers, his hands slid down over the curve of her body and held her close against him, sensuously making her feel the potency of his arousal. Her head tipped back as she struggled to breathe, hot desire constricting her throat.

His eyes seared into hers. 'You're mine, Lauren,' he muttered harshly, 'and you'll be a good deal safer if you don't forget it!'

For one tense moment they hovered between the twin fires of anger and passion, but at last drew back from confronting either. He let her go, and she stepped back, her arms hugging her waist as if she could control thus the churning emotions that raged inside her. 'I've waited a long time for you, Lauren,' he warned her in a voice still smoky from the fires that raged in his eyes. 'I'm not prepared to wait a moment longer than I have to. If you want it to be legal first, we get a special licence.' Lauren gasped with shock. 'You've said you'll marry me,' he went on, his eyes glittering fiercely, 'and I'm not going to let you change your mind. I don't know what's going on inside your lovely head, but I know what your body tells me. I'm never going to let you go.'

Abruptly he turned from her, cast off the boat and went to start the engine. Lauren gazed after him, cursing herself for being so vulnerable to his practised seduction. He knew exactly how to make her respond, as skilfully and almost as impersonally as he knew how to get the best from his boat. Under the full-throated roar of the twin British-built Sabre engines they were pounding over the water at a good thirty knots. Joe could have gone slower, relaxed and let the boat almost drive herself, simply adjusting for wind and current changes as necessary. But he chose to drive her at her top speed, putting her through her paces for the sheer exhilaration of being in control of something that wanted to resist him, wanted to wrench herself out of his grip even if it meant letting herself be dashed to pieces on the rocks.

Lauren watched him ride the bucking deck with effortless ease, watched his strong hands on the wheel, and shuddered. Whatever happened, she must never surrender to him. She had to keep her head, scheme and plan, out-manouevre him if she could. She daren't argue with him about the special licence—he was perfectly capable of carrying out the threat implicit in his words. Though it gave her only a few days, she would have to think of something to stall him when she was safely back on her own territory. Anyway, it would be easier to think away from his disturbing presence. For now she had to let him believe she was acquiescent.

Walking forward, she gave him a pleasant smile as she stepped down into the cabin. 'I'm going to make a start on that food,' she said as casually as if nothing had happened.

Joe threw her a puzzled glance, but chose to accept her manner without comment. 'I'll have a sandwich and a can of beer,' he said.

She brought them up to him, and sat beside him on the deck munching a tuna-fish sandwich. At that speed the whipping of the wind over their heads made conversation difficult, so she sat back and watched as the familiar scenery slid by. A school of flying-fish darted away from their wake. A dolphin swam with them for a while. The emerald-green cushions of the islands floated past—Mustique, Bequia.

In less than an hour they were at St Vincent. Joe nudged *Midnight Lady* into a berth at the Kingstown quayside, and Lauren jumped ashore to tie her up. The harbour was as busy as ever. A shower of rain had fallen a few minutes earlier, but already the hot sun was drying the ground with a shimmer of heat-mist. Car horns competed with the cries of children and the barking of dogs to assail her ears, and a thousand perfumes filled the air.

Joe took her hand to lead her across the busy road into the business quarter of the town, and she felt a strange little jolt of electricity at his touch. The main business of the afternoon was quickly accomplished, and if Joe was surprised at her meekness in the face of his high-handed behaviour he made no remark.

In fact her mind had been working in overdrive, but on another aspect of her difficulties. As they came out into the sunlight after their conversation with a slightly scandalised vicar, she said with studied casualness, 'I have some business to attend to now, Joe. Could I meet you in an hour?'

He gave her a look of swift intensity, but seemed to judge that with their wedding date set for just three days hence he need not cross-question her. 'Sure,' he answered easily. 'I'll meet you at the Cobblestone Inn—up on the roof-lounge.'

'Fine.'

As Lauren turned away he grabbed her arm and swung her back, and dropped a light kiss on her surprised lips. 'Be good,' he warned teasingly, and let her go.

She plunged quickly into the crowded streets, dodging through the one-way traffic of bicycles, donkey-carts and battered cars. She skipped over the muddy gutter up on to the high kerbs, and slipped into the shadowy coolness under the arcade, glancing swiftly over her shoulder to check that Joe wasn't following her. She didn't want to have to answer any awkward questions.

She eyed Mr McGuiness' grubby premises with

distaste. The fluffy young girl in the outer office had clearly not been retained for any brains that might lurk unsuspected behind her vacant face.

'Oh yes,' she responded with a fatuous giggle to Lauren's request to see the broker, 'I'll see if he's in.' Lauren smiled to herself as the girl pantomimed the efficient secretary, returning to hold the door open for her. 'Mr McGuiness will see you now,' she piped in her lightweight voice.

A wave of depression gripped Lauren's heart as she stepped into the cluttered office. She had little hope that Mr McGuiness would be much help to her. If her enemies put the slightest pressure on him he would cave in without a fight. But he was her only chance.

'Ah, Mrs Henderson. So very nice to see you again,' he bumbled, fussing around to clear a chair for her to sit on.

She clasped her hands together in her lap to subdue their shaking. 'Mr McGuiness, I'll come straight to the point,' she began. 'As you warned me, I'm being subjected to pressure from one of my creditors.' He bobbed his head in acknowledgement, his eyes flickering everywhere but her face. She could not dispel the suspicion that he had a guilty conscience. He was out of his depth in this evil world, she reflected ruefully, even more than she was herself. But she dared not go to the bank for help. As soon as they found out the situation she was in, they would call in her overdraft. They would never consider lending her more money. 'I think it would be best to re-finance that loan from another source,' she said tensely.

He nodded thoughtfully, and went on nodding, as if he had forgotten how to keep his head still. Lauren felt herself growing impatient. At last he said slowly, 'Oh dear. That might not be very easy.'

'I'm aware of that,' she snapped. 'No respectable financial institution will lend me money.'

He flinched at her angry tone. 'Of course,' he responded hastily, 'I'd like very much to be able to help you. But I'm afraid that with interest rates so high . . .'

'I need a quarter of a million dollars,' she stated flatly.

McGuiness looked miserable. 'Oh dear,' he said. 'Oh dear, oh dear. That's going to be very difficult. But I did warn you.'

'So you did,' sighed Lauren, controlling her irritation with an effort.

'Have you thought any more about selling?' he enquired earnestly. 'As a matter of fact, I've had a number of enquiries recently about investments in the leisure industry. Only a few days ago I had a call, and the Blue Lagoon was mentioned by name.'

Lauren lifted a finely-arched eyebrow. 'Indeed? Isn't that a little . . . convenient?' she enquired, unable to keep the thread of suspicion from her voice.

'No, no, not at all,' he flustered. 'It isn't really surprising that people should be wondering about your plans, since poor Bill's death.' He picked up a paper-clip and twiddled it nervously between his fingers. 'It would be a very good offer. If I were you, I'd give it very serious consideration.'

'I thought I had made it clear that I don't wish to sell,' she told him coldly.

'A pity,' he mumbled, shaking his head. 'I just hope no ill comes of it.'

Her eyes compelled him to look at her. 'What do you mean?' she asked insistently.

'Well,' he confessed reluctantly, 'there are some

people who don't like to see independent casinos operating. They see it as . . . untidy.'

'And you think they might try to force me out of business?' she asked a little nervously.

'It's possible,' he conceded, choosing his words carefully. 'The type of people who move in the background, buy up loans and mortgages . . .' His words hung in the air like a knife.

'Who has been buying up my loans, Mr McGuiness?' she asked, fear twisting in her stomach.

'I don't even know who they are myself,' he admitted unhappily. 'As I said, they move in the background, use innocent-looking companies to front them. But there's big money in this.' He leaned forward, and it was fear that she recognised in his eyes. 'I'm talking about New York, Chicago, Vegas. These boys play with the gloves off. Please, Mrs Henderson, sell out. Don't try to fight them. They're too big, they play too dirty. I wouldn't like to see you get hurt.'

Suddenly she felt terribly sorry for this poor little man. He was genuinely scared; someone had been putting the thumbscrews on him. She shivered.

'I can't sell out, Mr McGuiness,' she told him frankly. 'You know I'd be left with hardly any money. I have no family to turn to. What do you think would happen to me if I had to sell the Blue Lagoon? Where would I find a job? You know what unemployment is like here in the islands.' She took a deep, steadying breath. 'I have no choice but to fight. I can't possibly sell the Blue Lagoon. Now can you find someone to lend me the money I need, not too many questions asked?'

He hesitated, then nodded reluctantly. 'Very well, I'll see what I can do.'

'Thank you.' Lauren extended her hand, and the hand that squeezed it was shaking and clammy. 'Just one more thing. You said someone had enquired specifically about the Blue Lagoon. Where did that call come from?'

He looked at her in surprise. 'New York,' he told her.

Her heart thudded painfully. 'I see. Well, good afternoon, Mr McGuiness. I look forward to hearing from you.'

'Good afternoon, Mrs Henderson.'

Lauren was glad to get outside. She wound her way through the rush-hour crush, and walked quickly downtown to the old sugar warehouse that had been converted into a charming hotel. Joe was waiting for her at a table that overlooked the magnificent sweep of the bay, and the smile he gave her creased her heart. But the nagging fear inside her was rising to a crescendo.

New York. Who didn't like the untidiness of independent casinos? New York? Was she sliding deeper into trouble even as she tried to avoid Straker's threats? And who, exactly, in New York? Could it be Joe's friends? Could Joe be behind all this? Just how far *was* he prepared to go to get what he wanted?

Joe seemed to sense her suspicion, try as she might to hide it. He ordered her a daiquiri, and his eyes slid over her contemplatively. 'Would you like to dine here, or at my place?' he asked.

Lauren tensed. She didn't want to go to Hurricane Bay at all if she could help it. On his own territory he would be a formidable opponent. 'I'd prefer to dine at the Blue Lagoon,' she responded firmly.

He shrugged indifferently. 'Sure,' he agreed.

She sipped her drink, gazing out over the panoramic

view to avoid looking at Joe. The sun was sinking into the sea in a blaze of gold, bathing the sapphire ocean with its molten brilliance. When Joe reached across and took her hand she flinched away from him instinctively.

His eyes flashed darkly, but his voice was calmly insistent. 'Give me your hand,' he ordered.

Trembling, she obeyed him, and felt him slide a ring on to her third finger. She looked down at it in astonishment. It was a large and beautiful diamond. The last long rays of the afternoon sun slanted into its brilliant blue-white heart, striking fire. A deep thrill shimmered through Lauren, and the eyes that she raised to Joe's face were unguarded.

Just for that one moment, it all seemed real.

Joe's fingers closed over hers, and she looked at his strong, sun-bronzed hand enfolding her slender one. If only he loved her! If only . . .

Knowing herself to be far too vulnerable, she drew back into her shell, carefully recomposing the fragments of her mask and fitting it into place. 'Thank you,' she said in a calm, steady voice. 'I had no idea you were still planning to buy me an engagement ring. It's . . . beautiful.'

His hard mouth curved in a sardonic smile. 'That's just the first instalment, to assure you that I intend to honour my side of the bargain,' he told her, his voice freezing her soul, 'and I intend to see that you honour yours.'

It should have been an evening of magical romance, sailing home over the quiet water with Joe, his ring on her finger, the sky darkening to a deep mysterious purple. Joe drove the boat slowly, lounging back in the seat, his arm casually around Lauren's shoulders. It was as if they were both pretending. The moon rose

HARLEQUIN
❤ PRESENTS ❤

A Real Sweetheart of a Deal!

PEEL BACK THIS CARD AND SEE WHAT YOU CAN GET! THEN...

Complete the Hand Inside ➤

It's easy! To play your cards right, just match this card with the cards inside.

Turn over for more details . . .

Incredible isn't it? Deal yourself in <u>right now</u> and get 7 fabulous gifts. ABSOLUTELY FREE.

1. 4 BRAND NEW HARLEQUIN PRESENTS NOVELS – FREE!
Sit back and enjoy the excitement, romance and thrills of fou
fantastic novels. You'll receive them as part of this winning streak

2. A BEAUTIFUL AND PRACTICAL PEN AND WATCH – FREE
This watch with its leather strap and digital read-out certainly look
elegant – but it is also extremely practical. Its quartz crystal move
ment keeps precision time! And the pen with its slim good looks wi
make writing a pleasure.

3. AN EXCITING MYSTERY BONUS – FREE!
And still your luck holds! You'll also receive a special mystery bonu
You'll be thrilled with this surprise gift. It will be the source of man
compliments as well as a useful and attractive addition to your hom

PLUS

**THERE'S MORE. THE DECK IS STACKED IN YOUR FAVOR. HER
ARE THREE MORE WINNING POINTS. YOU'LL ALSO RECEIVE**

4. A MONTHLY NEWSLETTER – FREE!
It's "Heart to Heart" – the insider's privileged look at our most popula
writers, upcoming books and even recipes from your favorit
authors.

5. CONVENIENT HOME DELIVERY
Imagine how you'll enjoy having the chance to preview the roma
tic adventures of our Harlequin heroines in the convenience of you
own home at less than retail prices! Here's how it works. Every mont
we'll deliver 8 new books right to your door. There's no obligation an
if you decide to keep them, they'll be yours for only $1.75! That's 2
less per book than what you pay in stores. And there's no extra char
for shipping and handling.

6. MORE GIFTS FROM TIME TO TIME – FREE!
It's easy to see why you have the winning hand. In addition to all th
other special deals available only to our home subscribers, you ca
look forward to additional free gifts throughout the year.

SO DEAL YOURSELF IN – YOU CAN'T HELP BUT WIN

Remember! To win this hand, all you have to do is place your sticker inside and DETACH AND MAIL THE CARD BELOW. You'll get four free books, a free pen and watch and an exciting mystery bonus.

BUT DON'T DELAY! MAIL US YOUR LUCKY CARD TODAY!
If card has been removed write to: Harlequin Reader Service, 901 Fuhrmann Blvd., P.O. Box 1394, Buffalo, N.Y. 14240-1394

NO POSTAGE
NECESSARY
IF MAILED
IN THE
UNITED STATES

BUSINESS REPLY CARD

First Class   Permit No. 717   Buffalo, NY

Postage will be paid by addressee

Harlequin Reader Service
901 Fuhrmann Blvd.
P.O. Box 1394
Buffalo, N.Y.
14240-9963

like a huge silver dollar, casting a shimmering path across the inky sea.

The stars came out one by one, brilliant against the blue-black sky. Lauren glanced down at her diamond, sparkling as brightly as if it were a star that Joe had caught for her. A secret smile curved her lips.

But all too soon the dark silhouette of St Arnoux rose on the horizon, a land of shadows and lurking dangers to Lauren now. Her tension increased as they drew nearer home. The bright neon sign of the Blue Lagoon seemed like a wrecker's light to her now. She had never felt more unsafe. Somewhere the two Stoats were watching her, waiting for their friend the Snake to return. And meanwhile the card-sharp from England was eating into her profits, undermining her chance to save herself.

And Joe . . . what was he? She had known him for so long, but had she ever really known him at all? Who was the real Joe Daley? Once she had loved a man who was strong and gentle—she could love that man still— but had he ever existed outside her dreams?

She watched him covertly as he steered the boat expertly into the crowded quay. She could scarcely believe that he could be the master-manipulator, ruthlessly scheming to bankrupt her so that she would have little alternative but to sell herself to him.

But his words echoed in her brain. 'I'll own the Blue Lagoon, and I'll own you.' He had made his terms perfectly clear. The ring on her finger was a symbol of bondage. She had less than three days to break free.

The nightclub was filling up, and in the casino the tables were noisy with the lighthearted play of the amateur gamblers. Lauren wondered uncomfortably what time the Englishman, Bernard Evans, would arrive to begin his assault on her baccarat table. If she could only trust Joe, she would have asked him to watch for her—no one in the islands had a better reputation for being able to spot a trickster.

But instead she murmured to him, 'Excuse me, Joe. I'll just slip upstairs and change into something more suitable. I won't be more than ten minutes.'

Joe smiled lazily. 'When a woman says that,' he drawled, 'I don't expect to see her for over an hour!'

Lauren laughed, and hurried upstairs, determined to prove him wrong. She had a quick shower, and chose a dress of cinnamon-coloured crêpe-de-chine that glowed against her honey skin. With practised speed she renewed her make-up and knotted her hair into an elegant evening style. Swiftly checking her reflection, she hurried quietly down the curving mahogany staircase to the wide foyer.

As she crossed towards the nightclub she froze. Out on the terrace she could hear Joe's voice, quiet, as if he didn't want to be overheard. She moved closer, and flattened herself into the shadow behind the front door. '. . . leave tonight. I suggest you go back to Europe for a while.' She heard another voice reply, but so quietly that she couldn't catch what it said. Then Joe spoke again. 'Don't worry, I'll take care of that. There isn't going to be any more trouble here.'

The other voice spoke. 'Well, Mr Daley, your terms are excellent. It's been a pleasure doing business with you.'

Lauren clenched her hand so tightly it made her fingers hurt. The voice was unmistakably English, very calm and flat. Bernard Evans! She heard the two men say good night to each other, then she heard footsteps walking away. She held her breath, and a moment later Joe strode back inside and walked through the doorway into the nightclub.

Lauren let go her breath in a long sigh. So it was true! Joe was conspiring against her, trapping her, hoping to panic her into marrying him by confronting her with bankruptcy. Now that he had secured her agreement to the special licence he felt his victory secure. 'There won't be any more trouble here.' She twisted the ring on her finger in agitation. She should have known.

Maybe he was even behind the Snake. After all, she had no idea who Mr Straker really was; he might not even exist. For all she knew it could be Joe that was buying up her debts—in which case he virtually owned the Blue Lagoon already. A chill crept over her. Even if many of the stories about him were wildly exaggerated, many questions remained unanswered. And she had every reason to know that he had a ruthless heart. Seven years ago he had cheated her, and left her only losing cards.

But if he already held her debts, he could easily force her to sell him the Blue Lagoon. Why then was he insisting on marrying her? He could offer her his 'protection' as he had several times before, and she would be in such a helpless position that it would be difficult for her to refuse.

Because he wanted her to be more than just his mistress. Her past resistance had nettled his pride. Now he wanted to own her, body and soul. And once she was in his power, that would be just what would happen. Every time he touched her, even when he only looked at her in that special, intimate way, she felt her defences falling. Her body betrayed her at every turn. The longing to feel his strong arms around her, to feel his hands caressing her, to be possessed by him . . .

She shook her head resolutely to clear the images from her brain. Yes, Joe could make her love him again. But there would be no love in return. Desire, yes; possessiveness, yes. But no love. She clenched her fist. If she didn't escape now, she never would. One thing was certain: Joe was as dangerous as a barracuda. She must keep her head, think clearly.

Fixing her best smile in place, she walked across the foyer into the bar-room. As she entered, Joe rose and came towards her, his eyes sliding over her with possessive pride. The smile he gave her made her heart lurch, but tonight he would find no chink in her armour.

'You look like a million dollars,' he told her warmly.

'No wonder you're so keen to get your hands on me,' she returned caustically.

His dark eyes flashed warningly. 'You knew the terms when you agreed the deal,' he reminded her harshly. 'It's a little too late to back out now.'

Lauren shrugged her slender shoulders. 'Don't worry, you'll get what you're paying for,' she sneered. 'Shall we dine?'

For a moment she thought he was going to hit her, but instead he drawled lazily, 'By all means, if it will sweeten your temper.'

She turned away from him, and led the way into the smart supper room, where a quiet table overlooking the gardens and the bay was always reserved for her. The food was delicious—a refreshing jellied orange consommé, followed by lightly-fried flying-fish served with lime and tartare sauce. But the taste was ruined by the vinegar on Lauren's tongue. Throughout the meal she answered Joe's attempts at conversation with cool monosyllables, allowing a hint of disdain to creep into her voice. She knew that it was terribly dangerous, goading him like this, but if she could provoke him into losing his temper and storming out she was as good as certain that his pride would never let him come back and apologise.

'What's got into you?' he demanded impatiently. 'You're about as friendly as a rattlesnake tonight!'

'I'm sorry,' she responded acidly, 'I wasn't aware that friendliness was required of me.'

'It would certainly make life a good deal more comfortable,' he returned sharply.

'No doubt.'

'Are you hinting that I'm going to have to put up with this sort of treatment after we're married?' he asked coldly. She slanted him a look of calculated distaste, and he laughed harshly. 'Oh no, you don't, sweetheart,' he warned her savagely. 'That little game may have kept Henderson at bay, but it won't work with me. I know just how to take you in hand.'

'You think so?' she returned in a voice that came from outer space.

'I know it. Once I've had you in my bed for a few nights, there'll be no more of your haughty ways.' His voice sank to a husky growl, promising magic. 'You're all woman, Lauren,' he went on softly, relentlessly, seducing her. 'Don't try to run away from it. There's nowhere for you to run. No matter how much you try to deny it, your body was made for love.' He had taken her hand and was stroking it gently, his eyes holding hers with their compelling darkness. 'Don't be afraid, Lauren. In a few days you'll be my wife, and then you'll know just what I mean.'

This wasn't the way it was supposed to be going. He was winning again. Desperately she dragged her hand away, and stood up, blinking back the tears that were stinging her eyes. 'Leave me alone,' she cried raggedly, 'I don't want you to make love to me—I don't want to marry you. Go away!'

Joe stood up too, and grasping her shoulders spun her outside on to the privacy of the shadowy terrace. Before she could escape he had pinned her against the wall, and his hand caught her hair, dragging her head back so that her body was curved in a quivering arc against his hard length. His cruel mouth descended on hers, crushing her lips apart, not caring if he hurt her. His hand slid up the thin silk of her dress, insolently claiming the right to enjoy her body whether she liked it or not. But she was helpless to control her response. Her racing blood made her dizzy, and her bones were melting in the heat of his caress.

Joe knew he was winning, and lifted his head to gaze down into her hectic eyes, a soft laugh of triumph on his lips. 'Like I said,' he murmured huskily, 'once I've got you in my bed . . .' His eyes slid down to where her breast swelled proudly beneath the clinging fabric of her dress, the taut bud of her nipple betraying clearly her state of arousal. With one tantalising finger he traced the curve. 'So beautiful,' he growled hungrily.

So fiercely did she have to fight the weakness inside her that it was blazing anger that emerged. 'The only way you'll get me into your bed is if you drag me there!' she threw at him bitterly. 'You cheated me when I wasn't old enough to know better, and then you just walked away. You'll never do that to me again!'

Joe gripped her shoulders firmly, restraining her struggles, but he could not calm her rising hysteria. 'Is that what this is all about?' he demanded sharply. 'Are you trying to punish me for what I did to you?'

Lauren was shaking from head to foot, tears

coursing freely down her cheeks. 'I could never punish you enough,' she sobbed. 'I hate you!' She tore his ring from her hand. 'Here, take your damned diamond! Did you think you could buy me with that?'

She threw it at him, and it fell to the ground unheeded. He shook her roughly. 'Lauren, stop it! Listen to me . . .'

She knocked his hands away and backed away from him. 'Get out of here!' she snarled. 'I never want to see you again. If you ever come back here, I'll have you thrown out!'

He took a pace towards her, and she turned and fled, down the steps and across the garden, and into the dark shadows under the trees. She found herself running towards the hidden cove, and turned away, fearing he would find her there. She climbed upwards instead, high up the crumbling side of the ancient volcano, until the trees thinned and she emerged on to a rocky shelf and stood looking down at the lights of the Blue Lagoon and Hurricane Bay, divided by the shoulder of the dark lava flow that ran down into the sea.

Somewhere above her, hidden against the starlight, a nightingale was spilling his loneliness into the darkness. She leaned back against the cool rock wall and let herself cry, all the pain that Joe had seared into her heart boiling back as raw and stinging now as it had been seven years ago.

CHAPTER SIX

'YOU'RE a rotten spoilsport, Joe Daley, and I hate you!' Lauren glared defiantly into Joe's dark eyes.

'Shut up and get in the boat,' he ordered tersely. She tossed her black hair defiantly. He took a threatening step towards her. 'You're not too big to be put over my knee,' he warned.

And he meant it, too. She knew that particular expression on his forceful jaw. She stepped back hastily, all too aware of the faces of the boys behind him, still smarting from the humiliation of his tongue-lashing and more than ready to laugh at her discomfiture. Lifting her chin, she stepped with as much dignity as she could muster from the luxurious yacht to the small motor-launch that served as the resort's general runaround. Joe jumped down beside her, cast off, and spun the wheel to gun the launch fast away from the bigger boat.

Lauren sat down in a sulky heap. 'I was only going fishing,' she complained.

'Just you, and the three of them, eh?' he returned dryly. 'Haven't you got an ounce of sense?'

'I wasn't going to *do* anything,' she protested.

'Don't be naïve!'

'You've got a dirty mind,' she accused.

'It's a good job for you that I have, kid. If I didn't look out for you . . .'

'I'm not a kid!'

'Then you should have known better,' he returned with infuriating logic.

'I hate you!'

'You said that.'

Lauren sulked all the way back to the Blue Lagoon, though she didn't really want to. It was a beautiful day to be out on the water. The sky was a perfect dome of porcelain blue, the sea a swathe of turquoise silk, the warm south-easterly trade wind stirred her black hair around her slim brown shoulders. And she was with Joe. Ah, happiness of happiness!

But Joe was angry with her, just for going out fishing with those three young men who were staying at her father's resort on their yacht. And she felt so humiliated that she didn't know how to apologise. Because Joe had been right. As soon as they'd got away from the shelter of the lagoon their manner towards her had undergone a subtle but rather frightening change. She'd just been wondering how on earth she was going to handle the situation when Joe had shown up to rescue her.

She looked up at his broad, impassive back as he steered the small craft swiftly and safely among the water-skiers and inexpert yachtsmen crowding the bay. He docked at the quayside among the luxury yachts and cabin cruisers, and helped Lauren up on to the wooden jetty.

The touch of his hand on her arm sent a small shiver through her. She swallowed hard, and said in a small voice, 'I'm sorry, Joe.'

He turned her to face him, and lifted her chin with one finger. 'They gave you a fright, didn't they, kid?' She nodded, forgetting to object to the hated epithet. 'If you want to go out fishing, I'll take you.'

Her heart rose at once. 'Will you, Joe?' she breathed excitedly, all her eagerness alight in her black eyes. 'When?'

That strange guarded expression that always puzzled her came into his eyes. 'I don't know,' he said evasively. 'When I can find the time.'

'Oh, Joe!' she pouted.

He grinned at her. 'Come on, kid, come and give me a hand in the office,' he suggested.

'I wish you wouldn't keep calling me kid,' she grumbled, but smiling now. 'I'm nearly eighteen.'

'So you are,' he laughed.

Lauren had been crazy about Joe for months. But he always treated her like a kid sister. She kept trying to tell herself that that was all she could expect—after all, he was so much older than her, and there were plenty of women chasing him. The head of the field at the moment was said to be the pert little blonde who helped out behind the bar, but a sassy redhead, one of the baccarat widows, was also attracting his interest. Lauren knew she had little hope of competing. But she had his friendship, and that she cherished, trying to make herself believe it was enough.

They strolled up through the bright gardens, and Lauren raced Joe up the steps of the terrace, two at a time, laughing, the dignity she had claimed for her seventeen years forgotten.

'What do you want me to do?' she asked as they walked up the private staircase from the nightclub to the office that overlooked the empty casino.

'Help me check the books. The auditors are coming next week,' he said, a frown darkening his brow. Lauren knew why he was worried. The Blue Lagoon ought to be doing well. That it wasn't, she knew, was her father's fault. Since her mother's death he had sought consolation more and more in his brandy bottle, and the resort had run heavily into debt. Things had been a little better since Joe had arrived three years ago to run the casino her father had decided to open. Now he virtually managed the whole place. But the repayments on the mortgages ate a big hole in the profits.

Joe got out the big ledgers, and for the next few hours they worked steadily. Lauren enjoyed chasing the elusive dollars through the columns of figures until she could pounce with glee on the original error, and balance the books.

'There!' sighed Joe at last. 'I think that about wraps it up.' He leaned back in his chair, stretching his arms to ease the tightness of the muscles in his wide shoulders. He smiled at Lauren, that slow, lazy smile that made her heart patter deliciously. 'Now, would the efficient secretary like to fetch her boss a cup of coffee?'

'Yes, sir,' she responded, play-acting gravely. 'Will there be anything else?'

'Not at present.' His eyes flickered down over her. She was wearing a white T-shirt and a pair of very brief shorts that revealed the maturing curves of her body, and with a thrill of excitement she recognised approval in those usually unfathomable dark eyes.

She laughed softly, not realising how the thoughts in her brain lowered the timbre of her voice seductively. 'If I really were your secretary, we'd be having a torrid affair,' she said daringly.

'What would you know about torrid affairs? teased Joe, his dark eyes gleaming devilishly.

Lauren's heart was racing. 'If I were your secretary, I'd show you,' she replied in artless challenge.

He pushed his chair back from the desk and patted his knee. 'Take a letter, Miss Holding,' he invited mockingly.

Quivering with emotions she barely understood,

Lauren rose to her feet. 'All right,' she responded in a voice that was little more than a whisper as she moved slowly round the desk towards him. Her eyes never left his. There was a potent spell in that mesmeric gaze, but was he the spellbinder, or was she?

As she sank on to his lap she was aware of a tension in him that matched her own. She put her arms around his neck, liking the way his big hands spanned her waist. He was in full control of how close he was going to allow her to get, but his glinting eyes mocked her to finish what she had started. She returned that look, imitating the sassy redhead's slanting gaze.

And then she leaned towards him and put her lips against his. His mouth felt warm and firm, and she pressed harder, the way she'd seen actors in films kiss. She closed her eyes, hardly able to believe that she was here in Joe's arms.

But he held her away from him, and a low laugh chuckled in his throat. 'That isn't how it's done,' he told her, his voice whispering soft. He lifted his hand and laid it along her cheek, and his thumb brushed across her lips, parting them a little. Then he drew her head down, and she felt his mouth against hers again, but this time it was different. This time there was a heat that scorched right through her, and his lips slid over hers, touching delicate membranes and making her body shimmer in response.

His arms tightened around her, tipping her back across his lap, and the kiss deepened and became more demanding. Lauren's head was dizzy with the racing of her blood. She was clinging to him as if she were falling, yielding to him all that he asked. Swirling darkness surrounded her like warm velvet, the musky maleness of his body assailing her senses. When he drew back she reached for him, sobbing his name on strangled breaths.

'Let me go, Lauren,' he commanded, his voice as rough as river-bed gravel. 'For God's sake get out of here!'

'You want me to go?' she whispered desperately, tears sparkling like diamonds on her thick black lashes.

He closed his eyes and groaned, as if in pain. 'Yes, I want you to go.'

She recognised the conflict in him, but not the roots from which it sprang. 'No, you don't,' she cried in innocent triumph, 'you want me to stay!'

Joe took her wrists in an iron grip and dragged her arms from round his neck. 'Listen, kid,' he rasped harshly, 'I've been trying to get it across to you for weeks. I'm not interested in your juvenile games!'

She laughed up at him provocatively. 'If that's what you're like when you're not interested, I'd like to be around when you start to get warmed up,' she said boldly.

'Well, you won't be,' he said cruelly, standing up and depositing her in an undignified heap on the floor.

Lauren sat up, hugging her knees, watching as he walked over to stare out of the window down into the well of the gaming room. Instinct told her that he was not as uninterested as he was pretending to be, but it told her no more, and she was puzzled and confused. 'Don't you like me, Joe?' she asked plaintively.

She saw him clench his fist. 'Run away, Lauren,' he said, almost to himself. 'Run away as fast as you can. Come back in a few years, when you've grown up, and then ask me if I like you.'

Something impassive in the line of his back told her that he wouldn't turn from the window until she was gone, so reluctantly she got to her feet and trailed from the room. 'I'm running, then,' she said over her shoulder as she walked through the door. 'But not very fast. You can catch me if you want me.'

For the next few days it was very clear to Lauren that Joe was avoiding her. With the folly of youth she saw this as a kind of triumph, and did her best to catch him alone. But he was too clever for her, and she had no chance to repeat what had taken place in the office.

But there was one place she knew she could always find him completely alone. At dawn, when the gaming room had closed down, and he had done the books, he would walk down to an isolated cove not far from the hotel, and swim and sunbathe in the solitude of the early morning. He never took any of his ladies with him. Lauren had often watched him returning, from the secrecy of her balcony, the sight of his lithe sun bronzed body stirring her senses in a way she was still too young to understand.

Sometimes during the day she would creep down to the cove herself. It was little more than a dent in the rocks, with a tiny beach of soft white sand shaded by palm trees and mangroves. It would be crowded if half a dozen people gathered there, but it was so well hidden by the tangle of trees that virtually no one else ever found the path that led down to it. The easier route lay across the island to Hurricane Bay.

Frustrated by Joe's avoidance of her, Lauren finally made up her mind to catch him out. So one morning she rose with the dawn, and put on her favourite bikini. It was pink, and flattered her colouring perfectly. The top scooped low over her firm young breasts, making her feel very grown up. She threw a towelling wrap around her shoulders, and in bare feet hurried out of the hotel by a little-used side entrance, and ran down the rugged path to the secret cove.

The morning air was as fresh as champagne, and she ran lightly, skipping over the aerial roots of the mangroves that trailed across the path to snare unwary ankles. The beach was empty, except for a dark blue towel. Shading her eyes with her hands, she squinted out to sea. A black, seal-like head was cleaving the water about a hundred yards from the shore. She stood for a moment, marvelling at the power of his stroke that resisted the current and took him in a straight line from one side of the encircling rocks to the other.

Quickly she took off her wrap and lay down on the powder-soft sand, then laid her forehead on her folded arms. She closed her eyes and waited. She heard him approach, breathing heavily from his swim, and saw his long shadow fall beside her as she cautiously opened her eyes.

'What are you doing here?' he asked discouragingly.

'Sunbathing,' she responded pertly. 'It isn't a private beach.'

'No.' He bent down and picked up his towel. 'Why are you up so early?'

'I couldn't sleep.'

'At your age?'

'Why must you keep harping on about my age?' she demanded crossly. 'I'm not a kid!'

Joe gave her a warning look. 'You're a kid in my book.'

'You didn't think I was a kid the other day,' she taunted him.

He drew a deep breath, his eyes glittering with that dangerous fire that she found so exciting. 'That shouldn't have happened,' he rasped, 'and it isn't going to happen again.'

'Didn't you enjoy it, Joe?' she teased, innocently

delighted with the effect she knew she was having on
him.

He moved over to sit down on a rock, and began
scrubbing at his hair with the towel. 'Listen, Lauren,
and listen good,' he said in a rough voice. 'In a few
years' time, you're going to be one hell of a woman.
But you're not going to cut your teeth on me. So just
leave me alone, okay?'

'Why are you saying that, Joe?' she pleaded in a
voice that was shaking with the emotion in her heart.
'You wouldn't have kissed me if you didn't like me.'

Hardly able to believe what she was doing, she got
up, and crossed the sand to stand in front of him. He
sensed her approach, and froze. Lauren put out her
hands and took the towel, and began rubbing dry his
hair. Slowly Joe lifted his head, until he looked up at
her. His eyes levelled on the soft curve of her breasts,
hiding in the barely adequate covering of her bikini
top. Then he looked up into her eyes, and she saw
again that satanic glitter.

'Lauren,' he muttered, then as if he couldn't stop
himself he put out his hands and pulled her to her
knees, then gathered her up in his arms, crushing her
against the hard wall of his chest. His lips lowered on
hers in a kiss that was both violent and tender. She
yielded to him all the secret territories of her mouth,
arching her supple young body into his demanding
embrace, shivering with heat as his hands ran down
the length of her bare back. She wrapped her arms
tightly around his head, feeling the thunder of his
heart that warned of the stirring of desires that only
the brave should awaken.

Then those stroking, caressing hands began to slide
up her body, slowly, but with intent, and she began to
quiver with anticipation, sensing the increasing

intimacy of his touch. His fingers curved over the firm roundness of her breast, and she felt her breath stop in her throat. She buried her face in the hollow of his shoulder, and heard the roughened drag of his breath against her ear as he moved aside the fabric of her bikini. His fingers began to trace tantalising circles over the naked curve of her breast, and as his thumb brushed lightly over her tender pink nipple a shaft of hot pleasure pierced her brain, making her gasp.

'Oh Joe,' she whispered, her voice low and unrecognisable, 'I love you.'

It was the wrong thing to say. He froze, and his hands moved to grip her shoulders and hold her away from him. His eyes scorched into hers. 'Listen, kid,' he rasped, 'this has got to stop, right now, do you understand? You're very nearly more than flesh and blood can stand...Oh, Lauren, don't cry!' He dragged her back into his arms, holding her head against his shoulder, gently stroking her hair. 'Don't cry, Lauren,' he murmured, his breath warm in her ear. 'You'll forget all this in a day or two, and everything will be back to normal.'

'I won't, Joe,' she sobbed into the hollow of his neck. 'I love you. I know you think I'm not old enough to understand, but it's the truth.'

'No, Lauren.' He took her face in his big, strong hands, and made her look up at him. 'You're far too young for what I want from you. You've no place with me. Don't you understand?'

Salt tears were streaming down her face. 'Please, Joe,' she begged desperately, not even knowing what she was asking for.

He gripped her shoulders and shook her fiercely. 'No, Lauren,' he rapped brutally. 'This is over, finished, as of now. Is that clear?' He snatched up his towel and tossed it round his wide shoulders, then he was gone, leaving her sobbing her heart out against the warm rock.

Joe had no need to avoid Lauren over the next few weeks. Shocked and humiliated by what had happened, she stayed out of his way. She spent a lot of her time alone, sunbathing on the terrace, and it was there that her father unexpectedly came in search of her.

'Ah, there you are, Lauren.'

She glanced up from her book. Her father was only forty-five, and he should have been handsome, but the inordinate amount of brandy he had drunk had taken its toll, and now his face was flaccid and his eyes dull.

'Hi, Dad,' she said dully. 'What do you want?'

'I'd like you to meet a friend of mine. Bill, this is my daughter.'

Lauren's eyes slid coldly over the man who was leering down at her. He was nearly the same age as her father, and he too should have been handsome, but there was a pampered softness about him that was vaguely repulsive. He was like a soft-bellied crab that needed the protection of a shell; and the shell, Lauren recognised at once, was money. From the handmade shoes to the thick gold chain round his neck, everything he wore shouted money.

'Well, hello there, Lauren. I sure am pleased to make your acquaintance.' He extended a moist hand, and Lauren shook it briefly. She thought that his attempts to make himself look younger than his years made him seem ridiculous, but she could tell by the watchful look in Dad's eyes that he was eager that she should make herself pleasant.

She smiled politely. 'Are you staying long, Mr . . .?

'Bill. Call me Bill,' he urged. 'I ain't got no specific plans, at present. I got no calls on my time, you unnerstand?'

Oh yes, she understood. The drawl was Texas, and the hint was oil. No wonder Dad was looking so anxious! She knew that the hotel was in deep financial trouble, and that Dad was hoping she might attract the attention of one of the millionaires who patronised the casino.

'Bill would love to see some of the island while he's here, pet,' Dad was saying.

Bill looked at him blankly, but then his dull brain caught up and he smiled broadly at her. 'Oh yes, I surely would, honey. I surely would.' His voice faded away as she stood up, and he looked at her in frank awe. She was slightly taller than him, even in her bare feet, and in the yellow sun-dress she looked like some exotic flower.

'There isn't much to see,' she said in a bored tone.

'Oh, I don't mind,' he responded a little breathlessly. 'I'm sure I'll find plenty to look at.'

Lauren glanced at her father, but he just looked vaguely embarrassed. She could expect no protection from that quarter, she realised with a cold little chill. Her head held at a dignified angle, she led Bill down to the stables and called for Scoot, the stable-lad.

'Harness a trap for me, Scoot,' she asked pleasantly.

'Sure, missy. I got one ready,' he answered brightly. 'Your pa sent word you was going for a drive.' He hurried away, and returned very quickly with a pony and trap. Lauren looked up in astonishment as he climbed on to the perch.

'You don't have to come, Scoot,' she told him.

'Yes, I do, missy,' he insisted. 'This here's an ornery pony. He won't clip for no one but me.'

'Well, why didn't you harness up one of the others?'

'They's all hired out, missy,' he explained in wide-eyed innocence. Lauren frowned. It was very unusual for *all* the ponies to be hired out. Maybe a party had gone trekking. Still, it would be handy to have Scoot along; she didn't fancy being alone with her admirer.

The pony clip-clopped slowly along the twisting road. The going was very poor. The steep slopes of the volcano were deeply gorged by small, swift-flowing streams, and the surface of the track was friable and subject to landslips. Lauren maintained a running commentary, obliging Bill to twist and turn uncomfortably in his seat to follow her pointing finger.

'Our volcano is extinct now,' she told him. 'It hasn't erupted during all the recorded history of the islands. Soufrière, on St Vincent, erupted only a few years ago, but no one was hurt. The worst eruption was in 1902, when two thousand people were killed.'

'Two thousand? Gee, that's terrible!'

'Oh, that was nothing,' she returned with wicked glee. 'Mount Pelée on Martinique blew at the same time, and wiped out nearly thirty thousand people in less than a minute. There was just one big ball of flame that roasted them alive, and it even sank ships at sea.'

Bill looked vaguely sick, and his eyes flickered nervously to the innocuous peak of St Arnoux. 'Are you *sure* it's extinct?' he asked shakily.

'Oh yes. Well, one can never be *absolutely* sure with volcanoes, of course,' she added blithely, 'but there are seismologists and things now to warn us if it starts to rumble. It's the same with the hurricanes,' she went on with gruesome delight, 'they can sweep in and flatten everything in no time, and toss people right up in the air and break every bone in their body. But nowadays they have early-warning systems, and they can nearly always tell us if a storm's on the way.'

Bill pulled out a handkerchief and swabbed his face. They had traversed the southern end of the island and come to a rocky bay, where dozens of boats, from small motor-cruisers to huge luxury schooners, bobbed at anchor while their owners made use of the exclusive facilities of the resort hotel that guarded this sheltered anchorage.

'This is Hurricane Bay,' announced Lauren. 'The English used to hide their frigates here when they were fighting the French, in the eighteenth century. They built the fort. It's a hotel now.'

They passed on, northwards along the steep Atlantic shore. The coastline on this side was blasted by the Atlantic gales, and there was little shelter from the trees against the high bright sun. Bill was soon sweating profusely, and by the time they reached the village he was more than glad to climb down from the trap to sit under the orange awning of the island's one café, which served also as general store, government office and local gossip-post.

Lauren sipped her fruit punch sparingly. The familiar aroma warned her that it was well laced with the potent island spirit. Bill soon recovered, and his sharp little eyes darted around the dusty open square between the brightly-painted clapboard houses and the rough wooden quayside.

'Why don't we go for a stroll?' he suggested. 'It looks nice and cool down there by the water.'

It was indeed an idyllic spot. The sparkling turquoise water met the long curving bar of blinding white sand with barely a ripple, and high palm trees cast a delicious dappled shade where they grew almost to the water's edge. It was a romantic paradise, but not to share with this leering Lothario. Lauren sought for an excuse not to go with him, when to her surprise young Scoot, who was sitting on the rough pavement close to their feet, piped up, 'Pony's getting restless, missy. We best be making tracks.'

Lauren glanced in astonishment at the pony, who had so far totally belied the evil reputation Scoot had given him, and now was peacefully cropping for weeds in the rough ground as if he would happily stay there for a week. Unexpectedly Scoot rolled his eyes in the direction of her chubby companion, and it was all Lauren could do not to giggle. She wondered who had put Scoot up to it. Her father? Or could it have been Joe?

'Oh yes, you're right, Scoot,' she said seriously, 'he can be pretty bad-tempered sometimes.'

Bill looked at the pony in alarm. At that moment a large bluebottle chose to settle on its nose, and it snorted impatiently. 'Oh!' Bill scrambled to his feet. 'Yes, well, maybe you're right, honey.'

Lauren turned from him to hide her laughter. She felt almost sorry for him. With the belt of his expensive linen slacks struggling to contain a slight paunch, and his hair a little unnaturally dark, he seemed almost pathetic. In her mind she had nicknamed him Buxom Billy.

The pony trailed patiently home, his head down, wondering why these stupid humans had to drag him out in the heat of the day, when any sensible creature would be enjoying a quiet siesta. He had a broad straw hat, with holes for his ears, that covered the back of his neck, and Lauren and Scoot were similarly protected. But by the time they got home Bill was feeling sick from the effect of the sun, and had to be helped from the trap by Scoot.

Lauren watched him go, her mouth curved with irrepressible laughter. Suddenly a familiar voice above her called, 'Hello. Did you have a nice drive?'

She looked up. Joe was on the terrace above her, leaning on the stone balustrade, smiling down at her. 'Yes, thank you,' she replied, trying to sound dignified, but the laughter broke out uncontrollably. 'But the pony was terrible ornery,' she added. 'He got so restless in St Arnoux that we had to come home, before he threw a fit and galloped away.'

Answering laughter danced in Joe's dark eyes. 'What a pity,' he remarked, 'and in the heat of the day, too. I do hope poor Mr Henderson hasn't got sunstroke.'

'Oh, so do I,' replied Lauren mendaciously. 'That would be too bad.' In the midst of her laughter she was uncomfortably aware that her cheeks were tinged with a soft pink and her pulse was skipping along rather too fast. But this was the first time she had talked to Joe since that morning on the beach, and she didn't want it to end too quickly. 'We had a nice cool drink in St Arnoux,' she went on artlessly. 'He's really keen to try all the local delicacies.'

Joe's brow darkened. 'Did he give you rum?' he asked sharply.

'Yes, but I didn't drink much of it,' she said. He was coming down the steps towards her.

'Good girl. You keep off the spirits. And maybe I'd better warn Mr Henderson to be careful how he samples the local delicacies. Some of them can be unexpectedly dangerous.'

The look he gave her held her motionless, her heart beating far too quickly. For a timeless moment they stood there in the sun-drenched garden, unaware of the cacophony of bird-noise or the brilliant hues of the bougainvillaea that tumbled over the white stone wall.

And then abruptly the moment was gone. Joe shrugged and turned away. 'See you around, then, kid,' he said lightly, and walked away round the corner of the building.

CHAPTER SEVEN

LATER Lauren saw her father, and he asked her the same question. 'Did you have a nice drive?'

'Not bad,' she returned indifferently. 'It was a bit hot.'

'Well, you did pick the worst time to go. Whatever possessed you to go out at that time of day?' he asked, ordering himself another drink from the barman.

'Mr Henderson seemed so keen,' she responded caustically, 'and you seemed anxious that I shouldn't disappoint him.'

Her father flushed, staring as if hypnotised into the rocks of ice in his glass. 'He's a nice man, Lauren,' he said despondently. 'You could do worse.'

So this was it. 'Could I?' she enquired doubtfully.

He lifted his eyes, and she saw all the bleakness of a life gone sour in their dull grey depths. 'You're nearly a woman now, Lauren,' he said, 'and you're going to be a beauty. Like your mother.' A tear of self-pity welled in his eye. He had truly adored the lovely young Venezuelan girl he had brought to the Blue Lagoon as his wife. When she died she had taken all the joy out of his life. So he drank. And then he would feel guilty for his neglect of their child, and so he would drink some more. He knew he had turned a successful business into a morass of debt. He owed it to Lauren now to see her right. He gazed at her mistily. 'You've got a valuable asset there, girl,' he said, more harshly than he had intended. 'Don't throw it all away on trash. Buy yourself some security.'

Lauren looked at him coldly for a long moment, then slid down from her bar-stool. 'Excuse me, Dad,' she said with as much politeness as she could muster, 'I'm going to get some supper.'

He caught her wrist as she passed. 'I'm talking about marriage, girl, if you play your cards right,' he rasped. 'What else is there for you to do now you've left school? I can't afford to keep you in idleness any longer. It's time you started earning your keep. Henderson's a rich man. Think about it—that's all I ask.'

She looked down at his hand on her wrist, then back up into his eyes, and he shrank back from the glacial glitter he saw there. Lauren turned and walked from the room. In five minutes she had grown up. She went to look for Joe.

She found him in the cellar, carefully loading the wine-racks with the latest shipment of young wine from France, laying it down to wait in the cool darkness until the right moment came for it to be tasted. He was wearing jeans and a sleeveless black T-shirt, and as she watched his smooth muscles move under the tanned skin she felt a dryness in her mouth.

One look told him that things had changed. Without a word he humped a couple of crates for them to sit on, and pulled out two bottles of beer, snapping off the caps on the edge of the wine rack. They sat opposite each other, sipping the beer, and he waited for Lauren to speak.

'Dad wants me to marry Bill Henderson,' she said baldly.

Joe wiped his hand across his mouth. 'Does he?' he asked slowly.

'Yes. Security, he calls it.'

'You say that like it's a dirty word.'

'Sometimes it is,' she said.

'You can do a hell of a lot better for yourself than Bill Henderson,' he said carefully.

'Dad reckons I can do a lot worse,' she said, 'like throwing myself away on trash.'

'Meaning me.'

Lauren looked down at her hands clasped in her lap. 'Yes, I suppose so,' she murmured reluctantly.

'He's right, you know,' he said gently.

She lifted her eyes to meet his. 'That isn't true,' she insisted with conviction. 'You're worth all of these horrid gamblers put together.'

Joe put up a hand and gently stroked her cheek. 'Lauren, I'm twenty-seven years old. I'm a mongrel from the rough end of Brooklyn, and I haven't a penny to my name except the wages your father pays me. And if he ever finds out you've been down here with me, he'll kick me off the island.'

'I'd come with you,' she whispered tensely, her eyes mesmerised by his.

He gave a brief, bitter laugh. 'I couldn't take you with me, Lauren. I'd be out of work. I couldn't look after you.'

'You could find another job,' she urged earnestly, 'and I could work.'

He smiled down at her. 'No, Lauren. You'd die of cold in New York,' he murmured, his eyes lingering over her face. 'You're so beautiful,' he went on, half to himself. 'You're growing up so fast you take my breath away.'

Her breath was warm on her lips, her heartbeat racing out of control, and when she laid her fingers against his hard chest she felt his heart thundering too. His hand curled around her head, drawing her closer, and with feral sensuality his teeth bit gently into the trembling softness of her lower lip. A shimmer of heat ran through her, melting her against him in pure feminine submissiveness, as he invaded the defenceless valley of her mouth, demanding all that she had to give. His hard hands held her in a quivering arc against the curve of his body, and the impact of his savagely aroused masculinity woke in her a deep hunger as fierce as his own, a hunger she knew that only he could satisfy.

His hand rose from her waist to encompass the firm swell of her breast, teasing the tender nipple into a taut bead, and the pleasure pierced her brain like incandescent wires. Her body was burning with a desire that she knew could consume her utterly if she let it, but fear of the flames drew her back from the very brink.

They parted, breathless, each hypnotised by the smouldering embers in the other's eyes. And then without a word. Lauren turned and ran from the cellar.

She cried herself to sleep, and woke early to find the bedclothes in a tumbled heap and a pearly luminosity in the sky. There was no sound from the casino. It was almost dawn, and Joe would be down at the hidden cove. The thought took her out of bed and on to the balcony. The warm breeze of dawn caressed her body through the thin cotton nightdress, stirring memories of the way Joe had touched her, the way he had looked at her, the way he had sworn as if cursing fate for putting temptation in his way.

If she hadn't run away from him yesterday, would he have told her to go, as he had before? She leaned against the stone rail of the balcony, watching the sun lightening the sky, painting a cloudscape of amethyst and grey above the shimmering jewel-bright Caribbean sea.

A single tear escaped from the corner of her eye and rolled slowly down her cheek. Joe had said she had no place with him—but he hadn't said he didn't want her. He thought he couldn't look after her, because he had no money, but she didn't care about money. She only wanted to be with him. She loved him with an intensity that hurt, her body ached with hunger for him. And he loved her—she knew he did. She had seen it in his eyes before she had run away from him last night. Once they had set the seal on their love, surely that would bind them together for all time?

Her breath stopped in her throat. If she went to him now, would he send her away, say that she was too young? She remembered the hot hunger of his kisses. No, he could not refuse her. Trembling, hardly daring to think about what she was doing, she ran across the room and pulled from her drawer her most exotic bikini. She had bought it in Bridgetown in a fit of daring, but she had never had the courage to wear it. It was no more than three triangles of black, held together by thin shoelace ties behind her back and over the slender curve of her hips.

She stared at her reflection in the mirror. Her critical appraisal saw a face that still held a hint of youthful softness, eyes that shone with innocence. But her mouth, which she had always thought too wide for beauty, looked different to her now. Joe had kissed her. She touched her lips thoughtfully with trembling fingers. No, he could not send her away. Quickly she threw a towelling wrap around her shoulders and hurried out into the sparkling dawn.

The sun had not yet risen above the ridge behind the Blue Lagoon, and under the trees the darkness was mysterious, but as she came nearer to the cove Lauren could see the shining water ahead of her, and the long rays of light began to filter low under the branches, lending a cathedral-like atmosphere to the noisy forest. A woodpecker was on the early shift, and a gaudy parrot was complaining crossly about the disturbance. A small blue heron, waiting patiently by a trickling brook, lifted his head and stood motionless to watch her as she slid past among the shadows.

He was there, swimming parallel to the shore, his powerful over-arm stroke making barely a splash. Breathless with excitement, Lauren let the robe slip from her shoulders and fall in a heap on the sand, then, savouring every moment of anticipation, she walked into the rolling surf. The water was not cold, but it was rougher here than in the still, leeward shelter of the Blue Lagoon, and she had not anticipated the strength of the current. But her body was young and strong, and she swam every day.

As the distance closed between them, Joe saw her, and stopped swimming, treading water as he waited for her to come close to him. She was out of breath from fighting the current, and had to put out a hand to his shoulder for support.

'What are you doing here?' he demanded roughly.

'I came to find you,' she pleaded.

'You shouldn't have come,' he said, but his voice wasn't angry, and his arm slid round her waist, drawing her close. 'You crazy fool, the current could have swept you away.'

'I didn't care.'

He turned her face towards him and looked down into her eyes, and in that moment Lauren knew that everything would be all right. 'You shouldn't have come,' he repeated, his voice vibrating huskily.

He swam with her until his feet touched the gently sloping bottom, then he walked, holding her in his arms. She wrapped her arms round his neck, clinging tightly. Joe carried her up the beach as if she weighed nothing, and knelt down with her in the warm soft sand. But still they held each other as if fearing to break the physical contact between them.

'I had to come,' she whispered, close to his ear. 'Please don't send me away.'

He buried his face in the hollow of her shoulder, and she heard his breath harsh in her ear. 'Oh, Lauren, I can't send you away, though I know I should,' he groaned unsteadily. 'I want you so much, I don't care what's right any more.' She was trembling uncontrollably, and his hands soothed her and aroused her with their slow, sensuous stroking. As if obeying an unspoken command she lifted her head to look up into his face. 'Don't be afraid,' Joe whispered softly.

She shook her head, her eyes never leaving his. He put up one hand to her cheek, stroking his thumb across her quivering lips, parting them as he had that first time he had kissed her. His fingers slid round to cage her skull, and he drew her up to claim her mouth with a hungry possessiveness that warned her that he had accepted her offer, and the time for games was past.

His tongue slid languorously across the delicate membranes inside her lips, re-kindling the embers of yesterday's passion, igniting fires inside her that she knew would reduce her innocence to ashes. But she was embracing her own destruction, dancing into the flames, thrilling to the power of the virile male demand she had aroused in him, and as the temperature mounted his arms tightened around her, crushing her against his hard length.

Her racing blood swirled dizzily in her head, and she knew he had laid her down. His hand stroked her stomach in slow, sensuous circles. Her eyes flickered open to look up into his face, and she quivered under the intent in his gaze as he watched her breasts rise and fall with the tumult of her breathing. Slowly he unfastened the ties that held the top of her bikini, and gently pulled it off. His eyes lingered over the soft fullness of her naked breasts, the tender rosebud peaks already tense in anticipation of his touch.

His clever hands caressed her with slow, warm sensuality, tracing tantalising circles over the curves of her body until she was almost sobbing with eagerness. He smiled down into her eyes understandingly, and closed her lids with kisses, chiding her gently for her impatience. But the kiss he bestowed on her hungry mouth belied his words, and she moved beneath him to solicit more of those delicious sensations.

His arms slid beneath her, moulding her pliant body to his will, and his mouth began to move down over the vulnerable curve of her throat, scalding her skin with hot kisses. A low, throbbing purr of pleasure escaped her lips. Joe buried his face in the valley between her breasts, the roughness of his cheek rasping gently against her silken skin, then he lifted his head to survey the enticing territory that lay naked beneath him.

'Beautiful,' he murmured almost reverently, and bent his head over her aching breast. His mouth closed over one taut pink nipple, making her cry out with the almost unbearable pleasure. Her whole body was pulsating with heat, and she moved beneath him in unconscious surrender. He returned to kiss her mouth again, plundering deeply in foretaste of the possession to come, and as his kisses strayed, down over her breasts, her stomach, her thighs, she began to tremble, almost afraid of the strength of her own hunger.

He moved back swiftly to lie above her, careful not to let his weight crush her, and as he gazed down into her face she saw in his eyes the reassurance of his tender care, and her fear ebbed into a warm tide of submission. She lay beneath him, yielding willingly as he coaxed her slender thighs apart, only the tiny bikini briefs protecting her innocence. He had already unfastened one tie, and as his hand moved to undo the other she reached up and wrapped her arms tightly round his neck.

'I love you, Joe,' she whispered as he pulled the scrap of fabric out of the way.

'I know.'

She wanted him to say that he loved her, but as he took her with cherishing gentleness, the joy of knowing that he accepted her love had to be enough.

Afterwards she lay in Joe's arms in the warm sand, drained of all but her love, blissfully exhausted as if she had battled the wild Atlantic rollers to come to rest in this paradise. She didn't want to move, not ever. Beside her Joe's breathing was peaceful now, his broad chest rising and falling in even rhythm. The bronze sheen of his skin was broken by rough dark hair scattered lightly from throat to navel, and Lauren couldn't resist the temptation to run her fingertips through those fine curls.

He stirred, and looked down at her. His dark eyes wore that strange, guarded look that she had come to know, and the first shadow of unease fell across her heart. 'I'm sorry,' he murmured.

'Sorry? But why?' Her voice emerged as a stricken whisper.

'I shouldn't have done that.' He stroked her cheek with a gentle finger. 'And you know it.'

Fear choked her, and she wrapped her arms tightly round his neck, burying her face against his rough cheek, unable to look into those fathomless dark eyes. 'It wasn't wrong, Joe,' she pleaded urgently. 'How could it be wrong? I love you.'

His arms tightened around her for a moment that was all too brief, but then he took her shoulders and put her firmly away from him. 'I know, kid. And I shouldn't have taken advantage of you,' he said.

Tears misted her eyes. She knelt in the sand, looking down at him, unable to believe that it was all going so terribly wrong. 'But, Joe ... it'll be all right. My father won't sack you when he understands. He'll let us get married, I know he will.'

Joe sat up, his hands resting on his knees, his eyes gazing out far beyond the horizon. 'I'm not going to marry you, Lauren,' he said flatly.

His words cut into her heart like cold steel. She had played her ace, and he had trumped it without a second thought. All she could think of to say was 'Why?'

Joe stood up, and picked up his towel. 'I told you before,' he said harshly, 'you're far too young. You'll grow up soon, and find yourself a handsome young millionaire who'll pamper you and adore you, and you'll forget all about me.' She was kneeling in the sand, gazing up at him, her face wet with tears, shaking her head slowly in disbelief. 'Anyway, I'm going away for a while,' he went on, brutally twisting the knife in her heart. 'Your father owes me some leave. I'm going back to the States, look up some old buddies, have a good time.'

'How long will you be gone?'

'I don't know,' he responded impatiently. 'One month, two. I might decide to stay there.'

'Take me with you, Joe,' she pleaded, jumping to her feet and trying to reach for his hands.

'No,' he snapped. He thrust her wrap towards her. 'Get dressed. We'd better not be seen walking back together.'

Lauren stared at him, utter desperation in her eyes. 'Don't you love me, Joe?' she begged brokenly.

His eyes were as black as the soul of Satan, and his voice as hard. One word. 'No.'

A tidal wave of despair broke over her, and she found herself running through the trees, dragging the wrap around her shoulders, tears streaming unchecked down her face.

Lauren opened her eyes, startled to find herself out on the mountainside in the darkness. Painfully her mind spanned the years, back to the present reality. Her face was wet with tears, and her body ached from deep inside with a hurt that she recognised all too well. She gazed up desolately at the distant stars. Would she ever stop loving Joe? After all that he had done to her; the lies, the deceit, the deliberate attempt to ensnare her into a kind of slavery, why must she love him still? Her heart twisted in pain, crying out against the cruel hopelessness that was all she could see before her.

If she had not loved Joe so much, marriage to him could have had a lot to offer—security, status . . . and a sexual relationship that would have sent the seismologists' instruments up here on the volcano into a flat spin! She could even have turned a blind eye if he had started to rove. But loving him, she could not live with him unless he loved her in return. That would be to tear a fresh cut into her heart every day.

But she had thrown his diamond ring back in his face, with a barrage of insults that he would never accept calmly. She shivered with cold fear. She had played the game and lost; now she could only await the whiplash of his revenge.

She couldn't face going back into the casino tonight; Raoul would have to manage without her. Slowly she walked back through the trees, to the tranquillity of the moonlit garden. But as she crossed towards the side entrance of the hotel, that led up to her own private suite, a shadow moved against the silvery grass, and she gasped in shock.

'Good evening, Mrs Henderson.' The silky tones were overlaid with an unmistakable Chicago drawl.

Involuntarily Lauren stepped back. 'Wh-what do you want?' she asked.

'I was expecting to see a friend of Mr Straker's here,' the Snake told her smoothly, 'but he ain't here. Seems like he must have been sent away.'

Panic and anger rose in Lauren's throat. 'Yes, he has,' she snarled ferociously, 'and if I ever see him here again I'll . . . have him thrown off my property! And you can tell that to your precious Mr Straker!'

'Mr Straker ain't gonna like it.'

'I don't give a damn what Mr Straker likes,' she exploded, 'and if he wants his money, tell him he'll have to get a bankruptcy order against me.'

'Now, Mrs Henderson, don't make me . . .'

'You got a problem here, Miz Henderson?'

Lauren raised startled eyes to the reassuringly large frame of Scoot, the stable-lad. 'Yes, I have, Scoot,' she said, her voice and hands trembling. 'This gentleman would like to be shown the shortest route off the premises.'

'I'm warning you, Mrs Henderson . . .'

'You heard the lady,' interrupted Scoot in a voice that warned that he would be happy to employ violence if the opportunity arose. 'You're leaving.' The stable-lad's large black hand descended on the Snake's shoulder, and he propelled him across the grass towards the quayside. Lauren stood shaking with apprehension. She was already regretting letting Scoot get involved. He was a big, strong young man, but the Snake's two unfriendly companions might know some tricks that his education hadn't extended to.

But a few minutes later she saw him walking calmly back across the garden. 'He's gone now, Miz Henderson,' he told her gently. 'He ain't gonna bother you no more tonight.'

'Thank you, Scoot,' she said, smiling with relief. 'Good night.'

'Good night, Miz Henderson. And don't you worry none—I'll be watching out.'

'I'm sure that isn't necessary, Scoot, but thank you.' She turned and climbed the stairs to her own apartment on the top floor.

She hated the sitting room. It was full of the expensive hi-fi equipment that Bill had bought for show. On the walls were some very ugly paintings by the latest fashionable artist. The room had been done up at least once a year by whichever exclusive interior designer was currently in vogue. That was Bill. Everything was display—there was no substance.

Seven years ago he had decided that an innocent young wife would be an amusing novelty, especially one who brought with her the dowry of a fashionable casino. Lauren gazed wryly round the room. If she had been taken for a fool, it was her own fault. The bitter memories mocked her.

*   *   *

Joe had left the island without even saying goodbye to her, and the one thought in her head now was to show him that she didn't care. How better than to marry someone else while he was away—someone rich enough to give her all the things that Joe could not afford? Her father was egging her on, dazzled by all Bill's fine talk of stocks and investments. And so she accepted Bill's proposal, and was married to him in less than three weeks.

Bill had been so careful not to alarm her with premature demands that even on her wedding night she had no thought of what her marriage meant. Buxom Billy was no more real to her than a cartoon character. While he was downstairs in the bar of the luxurious Barbados hotel he had carried her off to, boasting and toasting wih his yachting cronies, Lauren lay curled up in the big bed in the lush honeymoon suite, and her dreams were all of Joe. Where was he? Did he ever think of her, and remember sharing the dawn on their hidden beach?

A finger stroked gently along her cheek, and she stirred in the blissful dream, the warm sand beneath her turning to silken sheets. 'Come along, honey, shove over and let your husband get his arms around you.'

Her eyes flew open in horror, and the next moment she was fighting in wild desperation, her screams and struggles useless. She lay, sobbing with pain and humiliation, as reality invaded her mind and her body.

A few nights were enough to teach her that fighting was useless, and she adopted a cold, passive resistance. After a few days they returned to the Blue Lagoon, but there was no joy in her homecoming. The cases of elegant clothes and beautiful jewellery that were carried up to her room from Bill's chartered yacht only made her feel even more wretched and humiliated. Bill Henderson had bought her, as he bought his heavy gold jewellery and pungent cigars.

Lauren was shocked by the condition of her father. Even in so short a time he seemed to be sinking without trace into the bottom of a brandy-glass, and the hotel was in chaos. Bill shrugged indifferently, so she took over the reins herself. No one seemed to remember that she was only seventeen. She hid the truth of her marriage behind a serene mask. The weeks passed, and the memories of Joe became no more than a dream to which she could escape from the ugly reality of the man who snored drunkenly beside her at night.

CHAPTER EIGHT

LAUREN shook the unpleasant memories from her mind, and turning her back on the sitting room went into her own bedroom, and resolutely closed the door. She was so tired. Her hair was a mess, and the hem of her dress was snagged by the undergrowth on the mountainside. But with well-schooled discipline she went through her night-time ritual, brushing out the silken swathe of her hair, then, relaxed from her warm bath, she slipped into bed, loving the sensation of the cool cotton sheets against her soft naked skin.

But the past would not be so easily dismissed. In the ungovernable realms of sleep, her mind took her back to the night Joe had returned to the Blue Lagoon.

She was walking gracefully down the stairs into the foyer. The after-dinner guests were just beginning to drift into the nightclub. She was wearing a dress of oyster-coloured satin that clung subtly to her slender figure and left her shoulders bare. Her hair was dressed in a sophisticated style, and diamonds glinted at her ears and throat.

Suddenly there was Joe, standing in the wide entrance porch, gazing up at her as if he'd seen a vision. Lauren stood transfixed, one slender hand lightly touching the oak balustrade, as their eyes met and held, and the long weeks of his absence evaporated like morning dew.

Then one of the staff came out of the bar room, and

not noticing Joe, called up to her, 'Mrs Henderson, this wine order . . .'

Bill was behind him, his red face signalling one of his uncompromising rages. He saw Joe, and bellowed, 'Daley! About time you decided to get back here, I must say! Damn fine thing, a manager just taking off for months on end whenever he feels like it. You'd better get behind that bar and start sorting out the bloody mess this fool's got us into. I can't do it all . . .'

There was a silence like a four-minute warning. Bill suddenly realised that he'd gone too far, and his face went white. Lauren had a fleeting impression that an earthquake or a tornado was about to rip them apart. Joe stood in the doorway like Samson in the gates of the temple; if he had stretched out his hands he could have pushed the whole building over.

But then to everyone's surprise he simply shouldered his bag and walked calmly across the hall and up the stairs, taking them two at a time. 'I'll be down in half an hour,' was all he said. He walked past Lauren without looking at her.

Lauren was in the bar when he came down. She saw his reflection in the mirrored wall behind the displays of liqueurs, and stiffened. He came up close behind her, and she felt as if the heat of his body was caressing her bare back, though he didn't touch her. 'Good evening, Mrs Henderson,' he said with formal politeness, but the low vibrating huskiness of his voice stirred chords deep inside her.

But she had rehearsed this moment many times, never truly believing that it would come. She would not allow Joe to know how deeply he had cut her. The mask of cool poise that she had trained herself to adopt in the weeks since her disastrous marriage came to her aid. Thrusting back the desperate weakness that would have had her fall into his arms and beg him to take her away, she turned slowly, and her eyes met his, hers now as guarded against revealing her thoughts as ever his were.

'Good evening, Joe,' she said smoothly.

One eyebrow lifted a fraction, but nothing else ruffled the suave urbanity of his response. 'May I offer my congratulations?'

'Thank you,' she answered with dignity.

He lifted a finger and touched the diamonds that trickled from her small ear. 'Very nice,' he mused dryly. 'And very expensive.'

'Of course.' Her spine was a rod of ice, holding her rigid, chilling her against his nearness.

'You did well for yourself,' he remarked a trifle acidly.

Lauren inclined her head in assent. 'One does one's best with the assets at one's disposal,' she returned cynically.

'Does one indeed?' He laughed sardonically, and his eyes drifted down over the curves of her body, subtly outlined by the clinging satin, with something very close to contempt. 'And such assets!'

'Only very slightly used,' she countered with quiet venom, and was gratified to see him flinch. 'The millionaire didn't seem to notice.'

'Ah yes—the millionaire. Not exactly young and handsome . . .' His lips curled into a sneer as his gaze turned to her husband, drinking in a noisy group at the other end of the bar.

'But then a millionaire doesn't need to be young and handsome, does he?' she countered smoothly.

'No, I suppose not,' he mocked. 'Pity, though.'

'Ah, but money ages so well,' Lauren remarked sweetly. 'Which is more than can be said for trash.'

She turned him an aloof shoulder and walked away, not waiting to see the effect of that last rejoinder.

It was impossible to ignore Joe's presence, but Lauren was careful to avoid any situation in which he might find her alone. The running of the Blue Lagoon she returned entirely into his hands. She had expected trouble between him and Bill Henderson, but surprisingly there was none. Whether this was because Bill was afraid of Joe, and tempered his blustering in his presence, or whether it was because of Joe's granite refusal to be drawn into a quarrel she wasn't sure. But she was thankful for the comparative calm that reigned.

She endured her husband's attentions in silent resentment, and every morning as the rising sun paled the sky she would slide carefully away from him as he lay in stentorian slumber, and slip out on to the balcony, a light silk wrap round her shoulders, and as the pastel clouds rolled away to reveal the blazing azure of the Caribbean sky she would let herself remember another dawn.

But by the time she came downstairs, in the middle of the afternoon, all memories and regrets were hidden, and if her youth had been stolen, her beauty was enhanced by the serenity and charm that she spun around herself like a cloak of golden cobwebs, distracting the eye from the silver tears that were hidden unshed behind the darkness of her gaze.

Her eighteenth birthday was the excuse for a splendid festival. Her birthday present was a heart-shaped swimming-pool, built on a flower-decked and floodlit terrace beside the hotel. Lauren suppressed a word of protest as crate after crate of champagne was carried out to the poolside. Tonight was going to cost a fortune, and they could ill afford it.

Today she had learned the irony of the truth. Her husband was no millionaire; he had decieved her father with his plausible manner.

One glimpse of the contract for the swimming-pool had been enough for her to put two and two together. 'You've borrowed the money to pay for it,' she accused flatly.

'So?' he countered aggressively.

'Why?' she demanded, her eyes flashing fire.

'My money's all tied up at the moment,' he explained evasively.

'Not so tied up that you couldn't lose fifteen thousand dollars to Sheik Jabul last week!'

'You don't understand money,' he blustered.

'Oh yes, I do. Quite enough to understand that you're not as rich as you led my father to believe!'

Bill waved a threatening finger in her face. 'You just keep your pretty little nose out of my business,' he warned her, 'or you'll suffer for it!'

Lauren stared at him stonily. 'You don't frighten me,' she said scathingly. 'You're nothing but a cheap little con-man.'

He grabbed her arm and swung her viciously against him. His fingers dug painfully into her soft flesh as he arched her back across the desk. 'So what are you going to do about it?' he grated at her. 'I still hold the mortgages on this place, remember? If you divorce me, I'll see you and your father on the streets!'

She sneered up at him disdainfully. 'I'll leave you,' she snarled, 'I'll get a job and support myself.'

'Oh yes? Doing what? Women like you are only good for one thing.' He put his hand down to lift up her skirt. She tore herself away from him, a sob of horror bursting from her throat. As she ran from the room she heard his chilling laugh behind her.

Lack of money had not diminished Bill's extravagance one bit. The party was a lavish affair. The free champagne flowed like water, and there were three varieties of caviar, as well as a sumptuous seafood buffet. Steel guitars played softly as the guests danced among the tubs of orchids around the lapis-tiled pool. At midnight the sky was lit by a blaze of fireworks, a stupendous display of spinning lights and sparkling showers, the finest that had been seen in the island for many years.

As every eye was turned up to the sky, Lauren heard a quiet voice close behind her. 'Happy birthday, Mrs Henderson.'

She didn't turn. 'Thank you, Joe,' she said coolly.

'You really are all grown up now, aren't you?' he drawled, his husky tones caressing her.

'Yes.' It was all she could trust herself to answer.

'And is this what you want?' he asked softly. His fingertips were on her arms, stroking lightly up to her shoulders. She felt his breath warm on the nape of her neck, where fine tendril curls softened the elegant upsweep of her hair. 'Or is this?' She felt his warm lips in the sensitive hollow of her shoulder, and her whole body began to smoulder beneath his touch. Oh, it would be so easy . . .

With all her strength she fought against the wild surge of desire that was sweeping her away. 'You told me yourself to marry a millionaire,' she stated flatly.

She heard the harsh drag of his breathing. 'This wasn't quite what I had in mind,' he said.

'A millionaire is a millionaire. Nothing else matters.'

'You don't mean that.'

'Don't I?' she uttered coldly. 'A few months ago I wouldn't have done. But things have changed since then. Like you said, I grew up.'

Joe's fingers stopped their slow, sensual arousal. 'Have they? Have they really changed that much? Look me in the eyes, Lauren, and tell me everything's changed, and I'll leave.' So that was why he'd stayed. He'd come back thinking to pick up their one-sided affair where he'd left it. He'd had a shock when he found she'd got married, but he'd realised at once that she hadn't married for love. So he'd hung around, thinking he could lure her back into his arms—and how much more to his taste, a secret liaison with a married woman, than a fraught relationship with an impressionable and impulsive young girl.

The hurt inside her made it easy to turn and face him, and to resist the searching intensity of his gaze. 'Do as you like, Joe,' she said in a voice colder than outer space, 'everything's changed.'

For a fleeting instant his dark eyes blazed, then the shutters slammed down, and with a slight formal bow he turned and walked away from her. Lauren watched him go, and knew he was leaving. Her heart screamed to her to run after him, but pride held her rooted to the spot. If she became Joe Daley's mistress, she would be his slave, and that was far worse than the humiliation she had to suffer at her husband's hands. Because Bill Henderson's claim was only over her body. Joe would take everything.

She made an excuse to slip away early to bed. From below she could hear the laughter and music of her birthday party, but it was on another planet. She closed her eyes, yielding to the beguiling lure of memories and dreams of what might have been. If only Joe had loved her . . .

The door crashed open and her husband lurched into the room. His piggy eyes were fierce. Lauren sat up, clutching the coverlet to her throat. 'Well, well, so you're alone after all!' he sneered.

'Of course,' she flashed angrily.

'Such a dutiful little wife!' he rasped, coming towards her.

'Get out!' she snarled. 'I hate you. Don't you ever touch me again!'

A slow smile spread across his face. 'Oh no,' he said, his voice pure threat. 'You're bought and paid for honey. You don't deny me anything.'

The next day Lauren stayed hidden in her room, letting only Kassy, the maid, bring her some food. She kept the room darkened, but Kassy saw the bruises.

'Oh, Miz Henderson!' she breathed, tears of sympathy in her eyes.

'Kassy, don't tell a soul about this. Do you understand?' Lauren insisted. 'I don't want anyone to know.'

Kassy looked obstinate for a moment, but then she nodded reluctantly. 'All right, Miz Henderson, I won't tell no one,' she promised. And when she returned to collect the tray, she pretended not to notice that the small, very sharp fruit knife was missing.

But that night Bill got spectacularly drunk and fell off the terrace wall. He didn't kill himself, but he broke his leg, his wrist and his collarbone, and was laid up for weeks. He seemed to regard it as some form of divine retribution, because after that he never came near Lauren. She moved back into her own room while he was in hospital, and he never demanded her return or so much as attempted to cross her threshold.

But Joe had gone, disappearing without another word and leaving behind a fertile seedbed of rumours. Lauren took over the nightclub and resort completely; her father rarely emerged from his alcohol-induced stupor, and her husband, on his recovery, celebrated his reprieve from death by scraping the barrel of life. His wild parties increased in decadence, and he became bloated and ugly, a pathetic figure fawned on by his bought friends.

Four years passed. Lauren struggled to keep the Blue Lagoon going, and ignored her husband's behaviour as if she wasn't even aware of it. Sometimes she heard that Joe was in the islands, and even that he was visiting Hurricane Bay with a party of his high-rolling friends, but she never saw him.

And then her father died. The night before his death he had been sober for the first time in months, and had sought Lauren out as she took some air on the terrace in the middle of the evening. It was a particularly beautiful night. The moon was a thin crescent of silver against the velvet purple of the sky. Taking her hand through his arm, he coaxed her to walk with him in the garden.

'Do you know,' he mused, 'it's exactly twenty-five years ago tonight that I met your mother?' Lauren didn't quite know what to say, but in his mood of reminiscence he did not need a response. 'Ah, she was a beauty! Eyes that shone like the midnight sun. Since she went . . . Ah well, you know all that.' He walked in silence for a while, and then he said, 'I know I've failed you, Lauren. When you were little, when your mother died, I promised her I'd take care of you. I haven't done a very good job.'

'Dad, I . . .'

'No, let me finish. I thought I was doing the right thing. But I should have let you go where you belonged. Nothing has turned out how I expected. I was taken in. I thought you would have security.' He shook his head sadly.

'We were both taken in, Dad,' she said gently.

He squeezed her hand. 'You hold on to the Blue Lagoon for all you're worth. And you'll be taken care of, I promise you that.' He kissed her cheek, and walked away. Lauren stood in the shadowy garden and watched him go. In her heart she knew he had been saying goodbye, and she wondered if she should run after him, try to stop him. But he had carried his burden of grief long enough. If he wanted to lay it down, it could only be his choice. She walked slowly back into the light and noise of the casino.

Not long after that, Joe Daley reappeared, and took over Hurricane Bay. Under his hand it prospered so well that no one could believe he was entirely inside the law. But in spite of his success, the Blue Lagoon remained a thorn in his side, a reminder, it was said, of his humbler days. He took to coming over about once a month, sometimes alone, sometimes with a group of his big-spending friends. On those nights, Bill would play least-in-sight. It was the general opinion of everyone that he was scared of Joe.

Lauren treated him with cool reserve, hiding behind her careful façade, playing out the masquerade of being Bill Henderson's loyal wife. But sometimes, alone in her bed, her dreams would drift her back to a distant dawn, and the soft warm sand of a hidden beach. And she would feel Joe's arms around her, and hear him murmur her name: 'Lauren . . .'

CHAPTER NINE

'. . . LAUREN, wake up!'

She opened her eyes. For a bewildered moment, time twisted like a cobra. Was it then or now? And then the acrid smell of burning smote her nostrils. 'Lauren, get up, quickly! There's no time to lose!' Joe was shouting at her with harsh urgency. He snatched up the skirt and top she had been wearing earlier from the chair where she had thrown them when she had changed so hurriedly, and pressed them into her hand. 'Get dressed,' he ordered.

She scrambled out of bed, oblivious that she was wearing nothing at all. She shrugged the little blouse round her bare shoulders, not bothering with a bra, and dragged on her tiny lace briefs. As she wrapped the skirt round her waist she was already running barefoot to the door, tying the belt as she went.

Orange light flickered ominously against the walls. Joe was at the head of the stairs and she ran to him, her fingers fumbling to do up some of the buttons on her blouse. 'Not this way,' said Joe, turning back, 'it's too late—the casino's an inferno.'

'The safe!' she cried, trying to dodge past him, but he snatched her back.

'Don't be stupid! You wouldn't even get down the stairs.' He was right. From below, the sound of crashing wood and exploding glass mingled with the terrible snapping of the flames. Joe grabbed her hand. 'Come on, we'll try the side door,' he shouted above the noise.

Lauren ran with him along the corridor and down the back stairs, but before they could reach the bottom the thick black smoke drove them back. Choking and dizzy, Lauren almost fell, but Joe half dragged, half carried her back up to the top floor. She clung to him, sobbing with terror. The flames were flickering along the corridor, and the smoke made it hard to breathe.

'We're trapped!' she gasped, realising with a rising surge of panic that the fire was raging under the floor beneath her feet, and that the joists might collapse at any moment.

'We'll have to try a window,' he said, pushing open a door and pulling her into the room that she had once shared for a brief few weeks with her husband. 'Stand back,' warned Joe.

He dragged the cover from the bed, and using it to protect his arm and face, smashed the glass in the french window so that they could get out on to the balcony. But they were still two floors up, and the ground was a dangerous drop away. 'The roof,' said Joe quickly. 'If we can get round the back we can climb down over the kitchens and the stables.'

He lifted her up before she could waste time arguing, and she scrambled frantically for the stone parapet as he pushed her strongly from below. She reached it, and knelt there panting for breath. 'What about you?' she asked anxiously.

'Move along. I can get up there,' he said confidently. He swung himself up, using the balcony rail and the window frame with the agility of a rock-climber until he knelt beside her.

'Were you ever a cat-burglar?' she asked, laughing in spite of—or maybe because of—the danger.

'No, minx,' he smiled. 'Come on, get moving. Can you stand?' He helped her to her feet, and trying not to think of the thirty-foot drop to her right, or the inferno blazing beneath the roof on her left, Lauren hurried as quickly as she dared along the parapet.

At the back of the building the sloping roof of the kitchens permitted them to slither down to the flat roof of the stables, and from there Joe dropped to the ground and turned to hold out his arms for her. She jumped, and he caught her safely, barely swaying beneath her weight.

Behind her the roof caved in with a roar, and the flames leapt a hundred feet into the air. She stepped back in shock, reaction setting in quickly. Joe's strong arms went round her again, and she burrowed into him, seeking safety. He held her head against his shoulder, gently stroking her hair, as he had once long ago. Past and present swirled together in her distraught mind; she lifted her head, and their mouths moved compulsively together to meet in a kiss that challenged the heat of the fire blazing behind them.

Deep in the back of Lauren's brain a troubled thought stirred. It was the merest wisp of smoke, hard to catch hold of, but it drew her back out of Joe's arms. She looked up at him, trying to crystallise that vague disquiet into a coherent idea. Joe's face was grimed with smoke, his dinner jacket was torn, and his hand was bleeding. If only she could think . . .

He saw the suspicion that was clouding her eyes, and moved to take her in his arms again, but she stepped back evasively. 'Thank you,' she said, her voice shaky. 'You saved my life.'

'Lauren, I . . .'

'I have to . . . go and see that everyone is safe,' she said hastily, and escaped before he could capture her again. The staff were huddled in a wide-eyed group at the side of the hotel, some of them clutching a few pathetic possessions; one of the maids was sobbing pitifully, and the chef was scolding her.

Raoul hurried forward as Lauren approached. 'Oh, Mrs Henderson, thank goodness you're all right!' he exclaimed. He had on only a pair of red silk pyjamas, and Lauren realised with sudden surprise that above the tree-clad slopes the sun was rising.

'Is everyone safe?' she asked quickly.

'Yes, Mrs Henderson, we're all safe. No one is hurt.'

'What happened? Do you know?'

'No, ma'am—I was asleep,' he replied, his calm voice steadying her. 'Mr Daley raised the alarm.'

'What time was that?' she asked.

'Not more than a few minutes ago, ma'am. I closed the casino at five, and put the money in the safe. I went to bed at half past five, and it's now half past six.'

'So the fire must have started not long after we closed,' she mused, staring at the burning building. 'No one heard anything?'

'No, ma'am.'

'It must have caught hold very quickly,' she said thoughtfully.

'Miz Henderson, Miz Henderson, what about the ponies?' Scoot's agitated voice cut across her train of thought.

'The ponies?' She turned, bewildered by the intrusion.

'Yes, Miz Henderson. What if the fire should spread to the stables?' he queried anxiously.

'You'd better get them out,' she responded, trying to clear her brain. 'Get a couple of the men to help you. Take them up to the trees and tie them up out of the way.'

'Yes, ma'am.' He hurried away.

Lauren looked round dazedly. 'Penny, are you okay?' she asked Scoot's pretty young wife. 'Why is Emily crying like that? Is she hurt?'

'No, ma'am,' Penny answered placidly, 'but she spent all her wages on a new dress, and she forgot to fetch it out.'

'Oh. Well, tell her not to worry, the insurance will cover it. At least no one's hurt, that's the main thing.'

'Yes, ma'am,' agreed Penny, smiling confidently.

Lauren felt strangely detached, aware that her staff were all looking to her for support, but not sure how she was supposed to feel. Should she be relieved that she was safe, or upset that she'd lost the hotel she'd fought so hard to save, or should she be raging at fate?

She was aware of Joe approaching behind her again. He turned her round and calmly began fastening the rest of the buttons on her blouse. 'The fire alarm . . .' she muttered, half to herself. 'Why didn't it go off?'

'It wasn't working,' Joe told her. 'When did you last get it checked?'

'Last year, I think.' The smoke was in her head. She was still asleep, and dreaming this. Her mouth felt parched, and her eyes were stinging. She glanced down at herself. She was filthy, and her hair lay in a tousled mane around her shoulders. She pushed it back impatiently.

Someone was saying, 'It just went up like a bomb.'

Like a bomb. She turned back to look at the building. It was a furnace now, alight from end to end, flames and smoke belching out of every window. The fire had spread as fast as if the place had been doused in petrol. *No!* It wasn't possible. Who . . .?

'Who did this, Lauren?' Joe had taken her arm and drawn her out of earshot of the staff. She stared up at him blankly. 'Who started the fire?' He looked into her startled eyes, but she couldn't read what was in his; his guard was impenetrable. 'It wasn't an accident,' he said gravely, 'not with the way it spread so fast.'

She stared at him in dawning horror. 'What are you suggesting?' she asked carefully.

'It was arson, Lauren. Someone started it deliberately. Who?'

She backed away from him, her eyes wide. His fingers loosed her arm without resistance. 'You tell me,' she said in a shocked whisper.

'Lauren, you don't think that I . . .'

'I don't know what to think,' she said warily. 'I don't want to think anything yet.' She turned back to look again at the blazing building. This had been her home all her life, and now it was dying before her eyes. She'd been so happy here when she was young. A sudden vivid image of playing hide-and-seek with her mother—she would have been no more than five or six years old; she heard again the rich laughter, saw the glossy black hair, heard her father laughing at them both, happy.

Silently the tears started to fall, and when Joe handed her a big silk handkerchief she took it with muffled thanks. Slowly she walked round to the front of the building, not noticing the sharp gravel beneath her bare feet, hardly even aware of the guests who had tumbled out of their yachts and bungalows, many in their nightclothes, to stand and stare at the spectacle.

She stared up at the terrace wall where she had seen Joe that morning after she had returned from her drive with Buxom Billy—the same wall Bill had fallen from that drunken night after he had assaulted her in the assertion of his marital rights. The bougainvillaea and hibiscus tumbled down the wall to join the riot of colour in the flowerbed beneath. But above them everything was destruction. Tongues of flame were licking through shattered windows, the wide cedarwood front doors were buckling, and soon would catch alight. Everything inside was burning fiercely; the brightness of the flames seemed to dim the sky.

'Great heavens, Bert, this is just fabulous!' Lauren heard a voice say behind her. 'Go fetch the camera—I wanna get some shots of this to show Emmy-Lou.'

'They won't come out,' her husband grumbled.

'Sure they will. You paid five hundred dollars for that camera, and if they don't come out I want our money back. Now go fetch it.'

Lauren turned and gazed blankly at the staring faces. Someone touched her arm and said, 'Gee, honey, I'm real sorry.' Someone else said, 'Tough luck,' and a third, 'Ain't there no fire-fighting equipment in these heathen places? What if we'd all been inside?'

Beyond them the blue waters of the lagoon lay calm and untroubled in the morning sun. Lauren walked through the staring crowd, which parted silently to let her pass, down through the garden and over the soft powdery sand to the water's edge. There she sat down, and absently watched as the tiny wavelets rippled around her toes, deliciously cool.

She was aware that Joe was standing behind her, about ten feet away, as if keeping guard over her, but she took no notice of him or of anything. She had lost—lost everything. Her creditors would have first claim on the insurance pay-out, and by the time she had paid compensation to the staff—they had lost everything too, including their jobs—she would be lucky to be left with a few hundred dollars.

She was totally at Joe's mercy now. If he didn't take her in, she would become part of the flotsam of the islands, earning her bread wherever and however she could. Would Joe still want her, penniless and destitute? And for how long? She had nothing left to negotiate for the security of marriage now. She would have to accept whatever terms he offered.

That unwelcome suspicion forced itself on her notice again. *No!* It wasn't possible. He couldn't have done that to her; she might have been killed. He had risked his life to save her . . . hadn't he? Doubts began to snatch at the fringes of her mind. *Had* he risked his life? Had fear and panic made the danger seem greater than it was?

Impatiently she shook her head, trying to clear the smoke from her brain. She didn't want to think about that—she didn't want to think about anything, only the diamond-bright sand and the sparkling water lapping her feet, as the sun climbed the sky to start another day.

'Lauren, the police are here.' Joe's voice drew her back from limbo, and she looked up to see the white launch, flying the flag of the St Vincent police force, nosing into the bay. Many of the yachts had left, and more were making ready to sail. The staying guests were leaving too, invited aboard yachts to sail on to the next stopping place.

'Shame about the Blue Lagoon,' they would say. 'Nice place.' And then they would forget about it.

Lauren leaned forward and scooped up a handful of cool water to splash her face clean, then stood up. It would take all her wits to survive now, with no cards left to play, but she was not prepared to concede defeat just yet.

She surveyed the desolation numbly. The sun was

high in the sky now, and the fire had almost burned itself out. Some of the ponies were loose in the garden, cropping the trampled grass indifferently. The staff were sitting round disconsolately on the steps of the terrace, a bedraggled and miserable group in their nightclothes and blankets.

The launch docked at the quayside, and a uniformed constable and two plain-clothes detectives climbed ashore. Aware of Joe still behind her, Lauren walked to meet them. 'Mrs Henderson? I'm Detective-Sergeant McKay,' the elder of the two plain-clothes men introduced himself. His voice was cultured, and his tone faultlessly polite, but there was no mistaking his air of authority.

'Good morning,' she said pleasantly, extending her hand.

'Ah, Mr Daley.' Lauren didn't miss the respect in the policeman's tone when he spoke to Joe, and instantly warned herself to take care. She could trust no one.

'Morning, McKay. Thank you for coming so quickly,' Joe said, assuming authority as calmly as if he were already the owner of the Blue Lagoon.

Lauren flashed him a cold look, and said to the policeman, 'Would you like to inspect the damage?'

'Aye, yes, let's have a look at that first,' he agreed; Lauren had the impression that he didn't really think it was necessary. As they walked up through the gardens he fell in beside Joe, and the two conversed in quiet voices. Lauren strained to catch what they were saying, but they were careful not to be overheard.

As she climbed the terrace steps, Raoul distracted her further with an enquiry on behalf of the staff. 'They don't know what they should do, Mrs

Henderson. They're hungry and tired, and they haven't got any clothes.'

'Oh dear . . . er . . . look, tell them to go round the bungalows and see what they can find. If we can get to the safe . . .'

'Go over to Hurricane Bay,' said Joe, coming up behind her. 'Gus will take care of all of you.'

'Thank you, sir,' said Raoul, smiling in relief.

Lauren would have liked to be angry with Joe, but she had to be grateful to him for taking care of her staff. 'Thank you,' she said reluctantly, but when he took her arm she glanced down coldly at his hand.

'I was going to suggest that you come over as well,' he said.

'No, thank you,' she said calmly, 'I prefer to stay here.'

He turned her round to face him, and his fingers gripped her shoulders fiercely. 'You're not staying here,' he told her sharply.

'Please take your hands off me,' she said glacially. 'We are no longer engaged, and you have absolutely no right to give me orders. I'll do exactly as I please.'

'You little fool!' he rapped harshly. 'You're coming to Hurricane Bay with me if I have to drag you there!'

'Kidnapping? That's illegal, you know. Or have you got the whole of the police department in your pocket?' she returned with a calculated sneer.

'All right,' he snarled, 'if you want it the hard way. But don't say I didn't warn you.'

He let her go, and she turned her back on him, rigid with anger and fear. She heard him talking to Sergeant McKay again, but she didn't even bother to try to listen. The policeman's examination of the building was cursory, to say the least. As they came round to the front after a brief look at the kitchens the staff were disappearing into the shadow of the trees on the path to Hurricane Bay.

'Didn't you want to question them?' Lauren asked impatiently.

'All in good time,' replied McKay steadily. 'I know where to find them if I want them.'

'I see.'

'Shall we step down to the launch?' he went on equably. 'We can talk more comfortably there.'

'By all means,' Lauren agreed acidly. She walked with dignity in spite of her dirty clothes, back down to the jetty. The uniformed constable handed her politely aboard the launch and ushered her into the small cabin. She sat very erect, her hands in her lap, her mouth set in a firm line.

Sergeant McKay came in and sat opposite her, his face suddenly very grave. 'Now, Mrs Henderson, if you're ready, I'd like to ask you a few questions.'

'Certainly,' she responded in a voice tense with annoyance.

'What time would you say the fire started?' he asked.

'About six o'clock. The casino closes at ... hey, why are we casting off?' she interrupted herself suddenly as the engine came to life.

'Please sit down, Mrs Henderson,' said McKay calmly.

'What ... where are we going?'

'To Kingstown,' he replied in a tone of utter reasonableness, 'to the police headquarters.'

'What for?' she demanded.

'We'd like to ask you a few questions,' he returned, unruffled.

'But ... we can do that here. I don't want to leave. I have to stay and keep an eye on things,' she protested.

'We'll send a couple of constables over.'

'Why is it necessary for me to go to police headquarters?' Lauren persisted, searching his inscrutable face.

'We'd like you to make a statement.'

'I can do that here,' she argued.

'I'd like you to accompany me to police headquarters, Mrs Henderson,' he stated impassively.

She stared at him in open-mouthed horror. 'Are you arresting me?' she asked in disbelief.

'Not at all, Mrs Henderson. You're merely helping us with our enquiries.'

The euphemism did nothing to reassure her. The launch was moving swiftly out of the bay. On the jetty, standing very still, his feet slightly apart, his hands deep in the pockets of his torn dinner jacket, was Joe. He just stood there, watching steadily as the launch rounded the headland and hid him from sight.

Lauren turned back to McKay. 'What has he said to you?' she demanded. 'Is he paying you? Is he trying to frame me?'

'Please sit down, Mrs Henderson,' McKay repeated in that chillingly calm voice.

Shocked and frightened, she sat down in the corner, drawing her knees up to her chest defensively, glaring at him. 'I won't answer any questions until I see my lawyer,' she stated defiantly.

He nodded, and promptly turned his attention away from her to the contents of his briefcase. She watched him, hating him, scared of him. The swiftness and ferocity of Joe's retaliation had left her bewildered. Gone was the cool and elegant Mrs Henderson; in her place was a wide-eyed, trembling waif, wondering what was going to happen to her.

As the outline of St Vincent appeared on the

horizon, Lauren sought to gather together the frayed threads of her dignity. 'May I have a comb, please?' she asked in an unsteady voice. Sergeant McKay put his hand in his pocket and handed her his own long-toothed comb. 'Thank you.' She pulled the comb through her hair, restoring some semblance of order to the tangle. She handed the comb back and said, 'I'd like to have a wash.' He indicated the small galley, and with a smile of sarcastic graciousness that was totally wasted on his indifference she stood up and walked into it. But as she tried to close the door he stopped her with his hand.

'It's all right,' she said coldly, 'I'm not going to try to escape out of the porthole. I'd just like to have a wash without a bunch of flatfoots gawping at me.'

He took the insult without batting an eyelid. 'Nevertheless, Mrs Henderson, please leave the door ajar. I'll retire to the other end of the cabin,' he told her, completely unruffled.

'Damn you!' she spat, and turned away from him, letting him leave the door how he wished. She stripped off her smoke-grimed clothes, ran herself a bowl of hot water, and rubbed herself all over with a bar of cheap white soap—there was no flannel, so she used her hands. There was only a thin cotton towel to dry herself on, but she scrubbed herself briskly, and felt better for the wash even though she had to put her dirty clothes back on.

As she stepped out into the cabin she saw that they were docking at the harbour. A crowd of children were swarming at the quayside as usual, boats were loading and unloading, dogs were barking. Lauren held her head high as she stepped from the launch, her cheeks tinged only a little with pink under the wide-eyed curiosity of the people. She was instantly recognised here in Kingstown, and the word of her arrest—or rather that she was 'helping the police with their enquiries'—would spread like wildfire down the islands.

She walked with the uniformed constable, looking neither to right nor left, and climbed into the police Land Rover with as much dignity as if she were going out to dine in her finest clothes. It was only a short distance to the police headquarters. The whole judicial system was a legacy from the days of British Colonial rule, and the police were exceedingly polite and efficient. But she was taken to a small, bare cell, with only a high leadlighted window, and she really began to think she was going to start screaming.

A pleasant young policewoman asked if she would like something to eat, and she said 'Yes' without thinking. When the food came she found to her surprise that she was very hungry. It seemed ridiculous to sit there, calmly eating salt pork and pigeon peas; she realised that she was in danger of becoming hysterical.

When the policewoman returned she said firmly, 'I want to see Sergeant McKay.'

'I'm sorry, Mrs Henderson,' the girl answered diffidently, 'he isn't available at present.'

'Then I wish to contact my lawyer,' Lauren insisted.

'Sergeant McKay will arrange that when he returns,' the policewoman said apologetically.

'I'm not under arrest, you know!' cried Lauren, her voice rising tensely. 'I can leave if I want to.'

'I'm very sorry, Mrs Henderson.' The girl took the tray and went out, and the heavy door clanged shut.

Lauren heard the key turn in the lock, and threw herself against the door, banging on it futilely with her fists. 'You let me out of here!' she screamed. She kicked the door viciously, forgetting she had no shoes on, and stubbed her toes painfully, but at least it gave her an excuse to cry. She curled up on the narrow bunk and cried herself to sleep.

She woke up when the door opened again, and sat up quickly, but it was only the young policewoman again. 'I've brought you some better blankets, and a sheet,' she said shyly. 'We don't usually get people like you in here, and I'm afraid it isn't very nice.'

'That it isn't,' agreed Lauren wryly. It wasn't fair to be nasty to the young woman—she was only obeying orders. 'Is Sergeant McKay back yet?'

The girl looked uncomfortable. 'No,' she said, 'he won't be in until tomorrow.'

'What about the Chief Constable?' The girl's eyes slid away. 'I know,' nodded Lauren dryly, 'Sergeant McKay will arrange it.' She looked dismally round the tiny cell. 'What's the sentence for arson?' she asked philosophically.

The girl looked startled. 'Oh, I don't think . . .'

'Five years? Ten?'

'It would probably be about five years,' the girl admitted reluctantly.

'Five years.' Lauren sat down on the edge of the bunk. At that moment she felt as if all the spirit had left her body.

'I'll fetch you some coffee,' the girl offered, backing out of the room, so much like one of Lauren's young maids that she had to smile. But there was nothing to smile about in her present situation. She shivered. Could Joe really be framing her? Could he make it stick? She wouldn't be the first to burn out a failing business to claim the insurance money. She was quite sure he could buy enough witnesses—she couldn't really blame them. Life was hard on the islands—a few thousand dollars could make a lot of difference. If the police were also in league with him, she was trapped. Alone in the tiny cell, she curled up on the bunk again and let the nightmares take her.

Time dragged more slowly than she had ever thought could be possible. When they brought her supper she thought it must be breakfast, and the night seemed endless. She was already wide awake when the dawn paled the tiny window, and by eight o'clock she was almost screaming with impatience.

The young policewoman came back on duty, and brought her some breakfast, but her request to see Sergeant McKay was politely blocked. 'Would you like me to wash your clothes for you?' she asked pleasantly. 'I'm on split shift today, and I could bring them back this evening.'

'Oh . . . yes, please.'

'I'm . . . sorry,' the girl said carefully.

'What? Oh . . . it's not your fault.' Lauren sighed. 'Would there be any chance of washing my hair? It's full of dust.'

'I'll bring you some hot water. I'm sure I'll be able to run out and get you some shampoo.'

Lauren smiled at her. 'Thank you.'

'I have to lock you in again now,' the girl said apologetically, 'but I won't be long.'

She brought a couple of magazines, as well as the shampoo, and for a while Lauren felt better, but the time soon started to drag again. The magazines were dull, and her head ached from not breathing any fresh air. She tried remembering poems she had learned at school, but they came out all jumbled up, and she found herself remembering instead her schooldays, and passing by the women's prison on a school trip up to Fort Charlotte. From its position it would have a splendid view over the bay—were there any windows?

In the end, the only thought left in her brain, still there after every attempt to drive it out, was of Joe. She gave up the fight and lay back on the bunk, and let herself get lost in dreams of what might have been. She had been given a coarse cotton overall of dark grey to wear—prison clothes. What would Joe think if he could see her now, her hair loose and unbrushed, no make-up? Would he be satisfied that he had punished her enough for defying him? Would he still want her? But he didn't come, and the interminable day wore away.

The policewoman came back and brought her some supper, but she wasn't hungry and could only pick at it. 'What's the time?' she asked when the girl came back for the tray.

'Ten to seven,' the policewoman said brightly.

'Is that all? I thought it must be at least ten o'clock.' If Joe had come then, she thought she would have killed him, but he didn't come, and as the evening wore on she began to admit to herself that he had won. There was nothing she wouldn't have done, however humiliating, to get out of that place. She would have begged him on her knees to take her away.

They put a drunk in the next cell, and he wailed for hours. Lauren paced around the room, measuring it with her hands and feet, calculating its size and area and volume, and how long it would take to empty if it were filled with water ... She sat on the bunk, hugging her knees, counting to one thousand, but she got lost in the middle of the five hundreds and lay down, still curled up in a ball, hugging the pillow and crying for Joe.

Images and memories swirled in her brain, and she

moaned softly to herself as her body felt again his caressing hands, his tantalising kisses, his hard possession. She knew it was folly to let herself think such thoughts, but she could not tear her mind into other channels. Dreams and reality mingled into an endless nightmare. By morning she was hollow-eyed and despairing.

The door clanged open, and Joe stood in the doorway. She drew away from him like a wild animal, terrified. 'Come on, Lauren,' he said.

'Where?' she whispered, wide-eyed and suspicious.

'Surely you haven't forgotten?' he said calmly. 'We're getting married today.'

Lauren shut her eyes tightly. So she had gone insane. It was the most natural thing in the world for Joe to have her locked in solitary confinement for forty-eight hours and then coolly remind her that it was her wedding day. 'No,' she whispered, shaking her head, trying to remember why everything was all wrong.

Joe stepped towards her, and suddenly she was screaming and fighting. But she was weak, and he overcame her easily, pinning her arms to her sides and holding her against him, talking softly to her in that treacherously caressing voice.

'Ssh! Come on, hush. Everything's all right now. I'm here.'

'What do you want?' Lauren asked in a shaking voice.

'I've come to fetch you. We're getting married, and then I'm taking you home.'

She stood rigid in the enfolding circle of his arms. 'And if I refuse?' she whispered tensely.

'You don't have any choice.' His voice was flat, ironed of all emotion.

'You mean if I refuse to marry you, you'll leave me

here?' she asked, looking up into his hard face without surprise. She turned slowly away from him, and looked round the cell. He was perfectly capable of carrying out his threat; he was completely ruthless. He wanted her, and he would stop at nothing to force her to do what he wanted. She shrugged her shoulders. 'Then I haven't got any choice,' she said dully. 'All right.'

'I'll tell them to bring your clothes.'

CHAPTER TEN

How many times had Lauren dreamed of this day? Standing beside Joe, his hand gripping hers as if to prevent her escape, repeating her vows in a small voice in the echoing stillness of the Georgian-styled Anglican church. She would not look at her daunting bridegroom, and yet her heart meant the words so deeply that she thought it would break.

If the vicar thought it odd—the bride, widowed less than a month, barefoot and tousle-haired, the groom with a face like granite, the only witnesses a detective-sergeant and a young policewoman—he gave no sign of it as he solemnly pronounced them man and wife.

Joe kept his grip on Lauren's hand as he thanked the vicar and the two witnesses, only letting her go when he had her safely aboard *Midnight Lady*. She sat in the cabin, staring blankly out of the window, as he steered the boat back to St Arnoux. He docked neatly in the reserved berth below the Hurricane Bay casino, then came down to the cabin and held out an imperious hand to her.

'Lauren,' he called quietly. She got to her feet and went to him—a zombie always obeys her master's voice. She let him take her hand and lead her up on deck and over the low transom-rail on to the wooden quayside. There was a flight of steps cut into the rock wall, and Joe drew her up them. The touch of his hand was strangely comforting, and she clung to it with both of hers, stumbling a little on the steep climb.

It was noon, and the place was almost deserted, an eerie stillness clinging to it beneath the high bright midday sun. The fortress had a forbidding aspect, hard and invincible like the man who owned it. He led her through the vaulted stone entrance hall, and she stood shivering in spite of the heat.

'Do you want to rest?' he asked.

Laurence shook her head. 'I'm not tired,' she said flatly.

'Well, would you like something to eat?'

'I'm not hungry.'

'What do you want to do, then?' Joe asked patiently.

'Nothing.'

He ran his hand back through his hair and sighed with resignation. 'Okay. I've got some work to do. Come up and sit with me for a while.'

Without a word she followed him upstairs to his private suite on the top floor. He had a large sitting room with a long balcony overlooking the bay. It was an uncompromisingly masculine room. The floor was of gleaming wood covered with richly-coloured Mexican rugs. The outside wall was of bare stone, the internal ones panelled with gleaming mahogany, hung with a set of unusual and original oil paintings by a Mexican artist. There was a large buttonback chesterfield of tobacco-coloured leather standing before a carved stone fireplace, and several deep comfortable armchairs. Between the two tall french windows that gave access to the balcony stood a huge, inlaid mahogany desk, littered with papers.

Lauren sat in one of the armchairs, curling her feet up underneath her, and stared out of the window. The bay had a rugged beauty quite different from the tranquillity of the Blue Lagoon. The trees clung to the steep rocky slopes with determination, twisted into gaunt shapes by the fierce Atlantic gales. Beyond the bar of black rock the sea was blue-grey, flecked with white. A lone sea-eagle was fishing off the headland.

Lauren's eyes shifted to Joe's wide back, his head bent over the report he was studying. Except for the tinge of grey at his temples, he looked no different now from what he had seven years ago. He was wearing dark blue slacks and a pale blue open-necked shirt, the cuffs rolled back over his strong, sun-bronzed forearms.

He didn't look right, stuck indoors on a sunny day like this, reading stuffy business papers. Lauren knew instinctively that he'd rather be out on the beach, skin-diving in the clear deep waters around the island, fishing for shark off his boat. She felt a sudden surge of longing to go over to him and massage those big, tense shoulder-muscles with her hands, tell him to leave his boring old paperwork and come for a swim with her.

She looked down at her left hand, at the slim band of gold that he'd put on her third finger, along with the big diamond engagement ring. She had married him. In a way, she admitted to herself, she had always known that she would. Joe was too strong for her, he was bound to win in the end. Soon would come the moment she had longed for and dreaded, all these years. He would demand a husband's rights, and she wouldn't be able to refuse him.

There was a tap on the door, and Joe called 'Come in.' A maid came in with a tray of coffee and sandwiches. 'Put it down over there,' said Joe, indicating a small table beside Lauren's chair. 'Thank you, Sally.'

The girl gave him a shy, half-inviting smile, and hurried out. Joe put down his report and came over to sit by Lauren. 'You'd better eat something,' he said.

'I'm not hungry,' she answered without spirit.

He picked up a sandwich and held it out to her. 'You'll eat,' he ordered in a voice that would brook no disobedience. Resentfully Lauren took the sandwich and bit into it. He poured her a coffee, sweetened it, and set it before her. He made her eat three sandwiches and drink the coffee before he was satisfied, and she was nearly crying with impotent rage by the time she had finished. She didn't dare resist him—she had seen too clearly in the last few days how swift and dangerous his anger could be.

But in spite of herself the food made her feel a little better—she realised she had eaten hardly a thing since the first meal in her cell. A light shower of rain had cooled the heat of the day, and she got up and walked out on to the balcony. The sun had emerged again very quickly and was drying the sparkling drops from the leaves. A rainbow hovered in the shimmering mist above the wooded slopes that surrounded the bay. It was a beautiful scene.

Lauren heard Joe step out on to the balcony behind her, and she stiffened. Nervously she took a few steps away from him, and he didn't try to stop her. 'I'd like to go for a walk,' she said unsteadily.

'I'll come with you.'

She turned and faced him. 'I'm not going to run away,' she told him.

He looked at her long and steadily. There was no expression in his dark eyes—no triumph, no possessiveness, no lust. Just a thoughtful watchfulness, as if he was aware that his conquest was not yet complete, and was waiting for that chink in her defences that would allow him to sweep in and claim her unconditional surrender. She turned away from him, back into the sitting room, and walked towards the door.

'You've nothing on your feet,' he said.

'It doesn't matter. I'm used to going barefoot.'

'I'd better take you to Bridgetown tomorrow and buy you some clothes,' he said. 'I'm sorry, I should have thought of it sooner. I forgot you've only got what you stand up in.'

'It doesn't matter,' she said again.

They walked in silence through the tangled slopes of creeper-clad plantains, twisted banyans and evil, poisonous machineels. Lauren took the path that led up the massive shoulder of the volcano, towards the dead crater. The way was steep and rough, but there was a strange satisfaction in driving herself on; she wanted to reach the very top, drive herself to the point of exhaustion and beyond.

She scrambled up the rocks, slipping in places. Joe climbed beside her, not even out of breath, catching her occasionally when she stumbled but not trying to stop her. Up and up she climbed, above the treeline, to where the slopes were bare scree, dotted with thorny shrubs and tiny bright wild flowers. The whole chain of islands was spread out, like pebbles tossed on the smooth dark blue surface of the sea. To the north the rugged shape of St Vincent lay on the horizon, a drift of white smoke highlighting the four-thousand-foot peak of Soufrière.

St Arnoux's own volcano was a peaceful thing by comparison. Little more than three hundred feet high, the crater was no more than a tree-choked hollow, where birds nested in no fear of disturbance from the cold magna core below. A little wooden hut sheltered the scientific equipment used by the geologists who visited regularly to check that the volcano's sleep was as deep as ever, but the local people knew that the birds would leave the crater long before the new-fangled equipment warned of trouble. But the volcano hadn't erupted in all the years there was any history remembered; its power was all diverted to Soufrière, grumbling to itself thirty miles to the north.

The warm south-east trade wind blew here straight from the tropics, stirring Lauren's hair and blowing long strands across her face. Her skirt tugged at her legs, and she had to hold it with one hand to stop it lifting. Joe had stretched full-length on the scree, his hands behind his head, his eyes closed. He was so still that he could have been asleep, but there was a watchfulness about him that warned her that he was aware of her every movement.

She sat down, and gazed out over the sparkling water. The sea-eagle was fishing again, hovering over his prey, then swooping with deadly precision and rising again with slow beats of his powerful wings to return to his nest high in the trees above the bay. Lauren lay back, staring up at the blue sky high above her head.

Joe was about five feet away from her. She could have rolled over to him, nestled into his arms, admitted that he had won. But she didn't. She lay and waited, wondering if he would come to her, and take her in the hot stillness of the afternoon. But he didn't.

'Lauren.' He was standing over her, his hands on his hips. Behind him the sun was sinking into the sea, turning it to a crucible of molten gold. 'Come on, it'll be dark soon,' he said tonelessly.

She got up, aware the breeze had blown her skirt aside, revealing her long slender legs. He walked ahead of her down the slope, and she wondered why he hadn't taken advantage of her while he had the chance.

What was he waiting for? Apprehension was making her tense. Soon it would be night, and the hunter would have his prey.

Early evening had brought the hotel to life. The staff were preparing for the influx of diners to the restaurant, and some keen gamblers were having a pre-dinner flutter at the roulette table. A dozen minor questions distracted Joe as they walked through the foyer and up the stairs, but he fielded them all with the same answer, 'Ask Gus.'

In his sitting room Joe dealt with his papers by stuffing them all into a drawer, then he turned round and looked at Lauren, who had curled herself up in her armchair again, hugging her knees as if to protect her body from threat. She was uncomfortably aware of a closed door ten feet behind her—his bedroom door. 'Shall we dine here or downstairs?' he asked.

'Downstairs,' she answered quickly, glad of the chance to choose not to be alone with him.

For a fleeting second she thought the mask of self-imposed restraint would crack, but with a slight ironic bow he acceded to her request, and offered her his arm. 'Will you join me for dinner, then, Mrs Daley?' he asked in a tone of bitter mockery. 'Since we're on our honeymoon I'm sure no one will expect us to dress formally.' Since she made no move, he took her hand and drew it firmly through his arm, and constrained her to walk with him back downstairs to the dining room.

A table for two was set in a quiet corner, next to an open window that looked down over the bay. Outside the night breeze was stirring the trees, and the sky was banking with inky clouds that drifted across the silver face of the moon. The meal was mouthwateringly perfect—a lobster cooked in creamy brandy sauce, served with a mellow honey-gold Montrachet wine. Lauren ate in silence, her eyes downcast on her plate, aware of Joe's closeness across the table and the steady passing of time.

A number of the guests, and even some of the staff, came up to the table to congratulate them on their marriage. Joe accepted their good wishes with relaxed charm, shaking hands and chinking glasses without embarrassment. Lauren sat uneasily, hardly able to lift her eyes, her cheeks blush-pink in the soft light. 'My wife has had a difficult time these last few days,' Joe would explain smoothly.

'Oh, sure, yes—the fire. Gee, honey, that was tough luck. Still, it's all turned out happily for you now.'

'Yes. Yes, it has. Thank you,' she would respond breathlessly.

And the guests would depart, shaking their heads. 'It's sure knocked the stuffing out of her. You'd hardly recognise her.'

'She was nearly killed, you know. He got her out in the nick of time.'

'Really? Gee, how romantic!'

They lingered for a long time at their table, sipping the rich Santo Domingo coffee as the restaurant emptied. Joe made no attempt to force her to talk. She gazed out of the window at the dark, windswept ocean and cloud-laced sky. It was so very different from the Blue Lagoon. It could have been a different island, though it was barely a mile away.

Something tugged at the edges of her mind, but she couldn't deal with that problem now. It was late, very late. Joe's hand had closed over hers and a hidden force compelled her to lift her eyes to his face. 'Shall we go to bed?' he asked quietly.

Lauren's breath stopped in her throat, and she

nodded. Joe drew her to her feet. The restaurant was empty now, the waiters moving noiselessly clearing the plates. Lauren didn't think she'd be able to walk, but somehow the touch of his hand gave her strength. They walked slowly through the lofty stone foyer and up the wide stairs, to his suite.

As the door closed behind her with a soft click she unlaced her hand from his and walked across the balcony. The fresh night breeze caressed her body sensuously, but the chill of fear had locked up her responsiveness. She felt as if she were cased in ice.

'Lauren.' She heard his voice, and turned. He was standing by the open bedroom door. 'Come here.'

Drawn by the hypnotic power of his dark eyes, she moved towards him, slowly, reluctantly, hugging her arms defensively round her waist. As she came close to him she lowered her eyes, unable to meet the intentness of his gaze. He reached out and drew her against him, his hand holding her head against his shoulder, soothing her.

But her wide, frightened eyes had seen the big bed, the rough handwoven coverlet of undyed wool thrown back. She stood rigid in the circle of his arms, and his warm breath could not melt her. He had taken her without love once before, and all but destroyed her. Now he was going to do it again. She knew that his clever hands would be able to coax her body to betray her, knew that her treacherous heart would make her cry out her love for him as he possessed her. He would take everything she had, drink her dry, then grow tired of her, as he had all his other women. But she would be trapped by her love and the ring on her finger.

A tear rolled wetly down her cheek. Without a word, Joe picked her up and carried her to the bed. He laid her down carefully, then kicked off his shoes and lay down beside her, fully dressed. And then he drew her into his arms, and pulled the rough cover up over them both, and cradling her very tenderly he murmured, 'Go to sleep, Lauren. You're quite safe. I'm not going to hurt you. I can wait a little longer.'

The faint male muskiness of his body invaded her senses, and the warmth of his gentle embrace slowly melted the chill in her bones. With a small sob she snuggled against him and felt his arms tighten around her. Her mind could not fathom what was happening, but she didn't try. She didn't fall asleep for a long time. Joe knew she was awake, but he didn't speak or move to caress her. He just held her, far into the night, and at last she slept.

She woke with the sun in her eyes. She lay blinking, slowly realising where she was, and why. She was alone in the big bed. Only the lingering muskiness on the crumpled sheets beside her reminded her that Joe had shared the night with her. She was still fully dressed. He hadn't touched her.

She slipped out of bed, and out on to the stone balcony. The sun was rising above the eastern horizon, turning the sea and the sky to iridescent mother-of-pearl. A little yellow breasted sugar-bird fluttered down to land on the stone pediment close beside her, bobbing his head comically, hoping for a titbit.

Lauren glanced back into the bedroom. The shirt and slacks Joe had been wearing were thrown across a chair, and suddenly she knew where he'd gone. Down to the secret cove, to swim in the solitude of dawn as he always had. Without even thinking about it she followed him.

As she hurried along the overgrown path she gave herself a hundred reasons why she was going. She was bowing before an inescapable fate. She was surrendering to him before he lost patience and took her by force. She was a zombie, obeying her master's unspoken command.

But as she stepped from the trees and saw him standing there in the sand, his bronzed body as hard-muscled and powerful as ever, she knew why she had come, why every choice she had made since Bill Henderson's death had set her free had led her to this moment. No matter what he was or what he'd done, she loved Joe Daley and she belonged to him. She always had.

He watched her walk across the sand, impassive. He wasn't going to honour her with seduction, or even force. He was waiting for her to offer herself in total surrender. With fumbling fingers Lauren untied the belt of her skirt, and let it float to the ground. Still he waited. She bent her head, her hair falling across her face as she concentrated on unfastening the buttons of her blouse. Then she slipped it from her bare shoulders. Her teeth bit into the quivering softness of her lip as she felt the warm touch of the breeze caressing her body.

When she looked up at Joe he hadn't moved a muscle. Only the blazing heat in his eyes showed that he wasn't carved from a block of mahogany. With a graceful movement she stripped off her tiny lace briefs and walked towards him.

As his eyes slid down over the naked curves of her body she felt the first nervous fluttering of desire deep inside her. But still Joe didn't move. She was close to him now, the raw masculinity of his body fascinating her. She put out a trembling hand and touched his broad hard chest; her fingertips trailed up through the rough smattering of curls, and over the wide muscular shoulder.

With bewildering suddenness the iron restraint shattered. His arms went round her, crushing her against him in a ferocious embrace, and his mouth took hers with an unleashed savagery that she knew was a punishment for keeping him waiting. His kiss was more of a conquest, ravishing every sensitive corner of her mouth mercilessly until she was melting helplessly in a warm rapturous flood.

He had lifted her off her feet, sweeping her up, and her head swam. Vaguely she knew that he had laid her on her back in the soft powdery sand, and her body felt the glorious weight of his, pinning her down, offering her no chance to escape from the onslaught of his fierce hunger.

His arm slid beneath her, lifting her in a quivering arc as his hand caressed her from shoulder to thigh with a rough gentleness that stirred her blood to white heat. His lips demanded all that her mouth had to give, and then wanted more, and she heard his breath harsh in her ear as his kisses scalded down over the vulnerable curve of her throat to trail liquid fire over her warm naked breasts.

His touch aroused the soft pink nipples to tender buds, and his clever fingers teased them, bringing a cry of delight to her lips, which changed to a throbbing sigh of ecstasy as the light tugging of his teeth and the hungry plundering of his mouth pulsed incandescent fire through her whole body.

Her fingers curled in his hair, and she moved beneath him, soliciting even more intimate caresses, but he was in no hurry now that he had her. He wanted every part of her—the smooth curve of her stomach, the silken inner softness of her thigh. The pleasure tortured her, tearing low animal moans from her throat as she writhed in the warm sand.

She thought she could take no more, and tried to escape, but he trapped her swiftly, demanding the surrender of her lips again, plundering the defenceless valley of her mouth with sweet, arousing tenderness. She was fighting him, the hurt and anger of years unleashed in tears and curses that made him laugh. Furious, she dug her nails viciously into his back, and his anger kindled in retaliation. He took both her wrists in one iron grasp and held them down in the sand, so that her body arched towards him in a vulnerable curve.

And then with unmistakable intent his thighs forced hers apart, and his eyes held hers with searing heat as he took her. His powerful body obliterated the last traces of her resistance, and she was one with him, rising in an upsurge hotter than any volcano, soaring and twisting and beating in the flames, climbing heaven's wings to explode in a fireball of heat and light that left her blind and melted and sobbing brokenly as with a last rasping drag of breath they fell, and he rolled away from her in the sand.

She felt him reach for her and draw her to lie against his chest as the pounding of his heartbeat returned slowly to normal and his breathing subsided to steady quietness. At long last he spoke. 'Why did you come?'

The dying of passion had brought reality flooding back with all the pain of life to frozen fingers. Their bodies had burned together in the same flame, but at the cooling they were still apart, separated by a chasm of fear and suspicion. Her voice was flat and lifeless as she answered him. 'I'm your wife, Joe. That gives you certain rights.'

He groaned, and rolled away from her. 'Oh,

Lauren,' he sighed, 'I didn't want it to be like this between us.'

She stood up, and began to get dressed, turning her back on him. He came up behind her and took her shoulders, arching her against him. His breath was warm in her ear as his mouth sought the sensitive hollows of her throat. 'It wasn't like this before,' he murmured huskily. 'You used to be in love with me. Don't you remember?'

Lauren broke away from him, keeping her face averted as she fumbled to fasten her blouse. 'Oh yes, I remember,' she spat bitterly, 'only too well. I remember how you used me, took your satisfaction, just as you have now . . .'

'Lauren, you came to me willingly, then and now,' he reminded her.

His words brought a soft blush of humiliation to her cheeks. 'I know,' she whispered. 'I haven't forgotten a thing.'

'Nor have I,' he said, his voice low and taut, 'though God knows I've tried. I come here every morning, and every morning I remember you as you were then. Sometimes I thought I'd go crazy, I wanted you so much. I would have killed for you!'

With a sudden heart-stopping chill his words brought to mind the riddle that had taunted her fuddled brain since the fire, and the solution slotted into place. Somehow she had thought that he would have seen the fire from the beach here, and could have run the short distance up the path to rescue her. But there had been something wrong with that explanation, something she hadn't been able to put her finger on until now. He had been wearing his white dinner jacket. He would never have come down to the beach in that. He must have come straight from Hurricane Bay. But how could he have seen the fire from there soon enough to get over to the Blue Lagoon before it took hold? The shoulder of the volcano would have hidden it from sight, and the distance over the rough road was more than a mile.

Slowly she turned to face him. 'And you nearly did, didn't you?' she whispered, backing away from him in fear. '*You* started the fire. You and your pride! You couldn't accept that I didn't want to marry you, so you tried to force me, tried to trap me. You thought that if I lost the Blue Lagoon I'd have no choice . . .'

'Lauren . . .'

He stopped towards her, and she stumbled back into the surf. '*No!*' she screamed. 'It was *you*! It's always been you.' She was rigid, trembling with shock. He caught her, and as she tried to struggle free his hand stung across her face.

But as she crumpled into a sobbing heap Joe scooped her up in his arms and held her tightly. 'Lauren, please listen to me,' he whispered urgently.

'No,' she cried, trying weakly to fight him. 'I never want to hear another one of your lies!'

'I've only ever lied to you once, Lauren,' he said, and his voice held such a deep note of sincerity that it arrested her momentarily, and she gazed up into his eyes. 'Here, on this beach, seven years ago. When I told you I didn't love you.'

All the world trembled in the sudden stillness. 'I thought I was doing the right thing,' he went on, and the hurt and pain in his voice at last told her that he was speaking the truth. 'You were so young. I thought you could have such a golden life if I didn't stand in your way. I never meant to make love to you, but I couldn't help myself. I loved you so much, and that morning when you came to me, so soft and beautiful, you took my breath away . . .'

There were tears rolling down Lauren's cheeks. 'You loved me?' she breathed tremulously.

'I've always loved you. Even when I wanted to kill you for marrying Henderson, I loved you. I used to watch you with him, and I wanted to break your lovely little neck with my bare hands.' His fingers slid around her throat, but it was he who groaned in pain. 'But I knew it was my own fault,' he admitted bitterly. 'You'd never have done it if I had been there to look after you.'

Lauren struggled out of his arms, still unwilling to accept what he was saying. 'Yes,' she sobbed angrily. 'You knew how much I loved you, and yet you just went away and left me. I didn't even know if you'd ever come back!'

Joe gathered her up, burying his face in her hair, and she could feel that he was shaking. 'It was the hardest thing I ever did, believe me,' he muttered almost incoherently. 'I stayed away as long as I could. I thought that by the time I got back you'd have forgotten me. I was sure there would be so many handsome and wealthy young men rushing to take my place. I thought I could just watch over you, see that you came to no harm, until you really fell in love. But when I came back, and saw you standing there on the stairs, I knew it was no good. I wanted you too much to step aside, no matter how wrong it was.'

His hands moved to grip her shoulders, and his eyes glittered fiercely into hers. 'And then I heard them call you Mrs Henderson. I'd have walked out right then, but it didn't take me more than five seconds to realise that you needed me more than ever. So I stayed, and I let Henderson know I was watching. I thought he'd taken the hint, until Kassy came and told me what he'd done to you.' He folded her back into his arms. 'So I threw him off the terrace,' he finished grimly.

Lauren gasped.

'Oh, I knew he wouldn't kill himself,' said Joe with a cold laugh. 'I warned him that if he ever laid a finger on you again I'd throw him off the roof.'

'He believed you,' she told him, an uncertain smile trembling on her lips.

'I know.' His hands were stroking gently over her back, up under the fine cotton of her blouse. 'I couldn't stay around after that, but though I left I was never far away. I knew everything that was happening at the Blue Lagoon.'

'So you did have the staff spying on me!' she protested in joyous indignation.

He nodded, smiling down at her. 'They hated him, you know.'

'With good cause,' Lauren said bitterly. 'He was a pig.'

'No one's ever going to hurt you again, sweetheart,' Joe promised, and sealed the vow with a kiss that was all tenderness.

They sat in the soft sand, wrapped around each other. 'Where did you go when you left the Blue Lagoon?' she asked curiously.

His eyes shifted away from her. 'I was afraid you were going to start asking awkward questions,' he said ruefully.

She reached up and wrapped her arms around his neck. 'Please tell me,' she pleaded softly. 'Let's never leave anything unsaid between us ever again. No matter what you've done, it doesn't matter to me. I love you.'

His arms tightened around her. 'Oh, I never did anything illegal,' he assured her. 'But ... well, you

remember Rick, that friend of mine from New York?'
Lauren nodded gravely. 'So I don't have to go into
details. Associating with Rick has got me a bad name
since I was six years old,' he added with a wry laugh.

'I bet you were a right little tough guy when you
were six,' said Lauren happily.

'I was. I'll tell you all about it one day.' He relaxed
back into the sand, drawing her down to lie on top of
him. 'Anyway, I once fished Rick's kid brother out of
the East River, and Rick is never one to forget a debt—
good or bad. To cut a long story short, he's got a lot of
important friends now—the kind who like to be very
discreet when they're indulging their vices. So I
chartered a big luxury yacht, and cruised it around the
islands. It was no holds barred. Rick put up the
bank—no limit, absolutely. I tell you, four years of
that was enough for one lifetime, but I made a fortune.

'Then one day your father came to see me, when we
were hauled in at Magda's.' His voice became grave.
'We talked for a long time. He told me that he'd had
enough, and asked me to look after you. I tried to talk
him out of it, but deep down I guess I knew how he
felt.' Lauren stroked the thick black hair gently back
from his forehead and kissed the corners of his eyes.
'So I promised him,' he went on. 'That's why I
bought Hurricane Bay from Magda.'

Lauren looked down at him speculatively. '*Was* she
your mistress?' she asked.

He laughed, deep in his throat, that rich, mellow
laugh that Lauren loved. 'No, minx, she was not,' he
chided her. 'If I'd had half the mistresses rumour has
credited me with, I'd never have had time to run my
casino!'

'But you have had women, haven't you?' she
persisted sadly.

'Yes, my love, I have,' he told her, his eyes gleaming with that devilish light that had always thrilled her. 'And more than I can count on the fingers of one hand. But none of them ever stirred my blood like you do, and now that I've got you I won't need anyone else. Not ever.'

He spoke with quiet certainty, and Lauren laid her head contentedly against his shoulder. 'Everyone said that you and she were lovers,' she teased.

'I know.' He chuckled. 'Magda was extremely amused by it. She was nearly fifty, and it tickled her enormously to be worrying about creating a scandal instead of counting her wrinkles! And as she so astutely pointed out, if we'd tried to deny it, the gossips would have only been even more convinced that it was true.'

'When did you fall in love with me?' Lauren asked shyly.

Joe laughed at her womanly curiosity. 'Remember that first summer when you came home for the holidays?'

'Joe!' She looked down at him, her eyes shocked. 'I was only fourteen!'

'I know.' He smiled reminiscently. 'You were all legs.' He began to trail his fingers deliciously down her spine, and she wriggled her body against his. 'I was twenty-five, and I felt like an old man. I was beginning to think I should get out of the whole rotten gambling racket, though it was the only thing I knew. And I'd never have got another job at the wages your father was paying me. But some of those rich pigs . . .

'And then suddenly there was this laughing kid, like a breath of fresh air. You were so lovely, I couldn't believe it. You were like those wild orchids you see growing all about the place, so delicate and beautiful, and growing up with no one to look out for you. I'll tell you one thing,' he interrupted himself abruptly, 'no kid of mine's growing up around a casino. When we rebuild the Blue Lagoon, it's for water sports only, right?'

'Right,' Lauren agreed happily, nestling into his shoulder.

'I dread to think what could have happened to you if I hadn't elected myself big brother,' he murmured, stroking her hair.

Lauren gurgled with laughter. 'You did, too. More than once I thought you were going to put me over your knee. I used to hate it!'

'Oh, you were a handful, all right,' he grinned. 'I used to see the way some of those guys looked at you. I made damn sure everyone knew I'd break the back of any man who touched you. You were so innocent, you just didn't seem to realise the effect you had.'

'I was only interested in you,' she whispered.

'I know. I began to realise it that summer you left school. I was running scared. I'd never had myself down as a cradle-snatcher, but I could hardly keep my hands off you. Then that day when we were in the office—one minute I was teasing you, and suddenly you were all woman.' His hand caressed her cheek, and his voice became serious. 'So in the end it was I who took your innocence away from you.'

'I was glad it was you,' she whispered, her voice trembling.

Joe hugged her convulsively. 'I'd be lying if I said I was sorry,' he said thickly. 'And afterwards—I nearly slit my throat every time I thought of you with Henderson. But at least I knew it had been me, the first time. He'd have hurt you, sweetheart.'

His fingers stroked her hair, running through its

silken length. 'I kept hoping you'd leave him, and come back to me. When you didn't I had to tell myself that it was my own fault, that I'd made you stop loving me.'

'No, you didn't,' she insisted urgently. 'I loved you all along. I thought you'd never loved me. I thought you just wanted . . . just wanted . . .'

Joe laughed huskily, and his hand moved to unfasten her blouse and brush it aside so that he could caress her breasts into warm arousal. 'I let you think it,' he told her. 'I wanted you to believe that that was the only thing between us. I told myself that you were no more than a cheap little tramp, who'd married an old man for his money.'

Lauren closed her eyes in humiliation. 'I only did it to spite you,' she whispered. 'I didn't want you to know how much you'd hurt me.'

'Oh, Lauren,' he murmured sadly. 'Such wasteful pride! I should have just taken you away, and loved you till you forgot how cruel I'd been to you. But I kept waiting, and hoping that in time . . . but time was what we didn't have.'

He stopped his idle fondling of her body and wrapped his arms round her, drawing her close down on to his chest again. 'I knew you were in trouble. I'd been buying up your debts for over a year, using one of Rick's firms as a front so Henderson wouldn't know it was me. And I guess that's where the trouble started. Rick's got some nasty enemies.'

'In Chicago?'

'Chicago?' He pulled her up, and looked at her fiercely. 'Vic Straker? You owed money to Vic Straker?' Lauren nodded dumbly, and with a groan of horror he buried her in his arms again. 'That bastard,' he muttered viciously. 'I might have known!'

'You know him?'

'Rick does. The two of them go way back. If Straker thought Rick was interested in you or the Blue Lagoon, that would have been enough for him to want to stamp you out.'

'I told his snake I had friends,' she admitted ruefully.

'You little fool. Why didn't you come to me for help?' Joe demanded harshly.

'I didn't trust you.'

He sighed. 'Yes, I knew that. I had to find out how bad things were, so I teased you into losing money to me. I could tell by your eyes that you were worried, and as soon as I got my hands on that fake diamond I knew it was serious. So I started hustling for the rest of your loans. That's when Straker started turning the screws, I guess.'

'Yes,' she said, shivering at the memory of the Snake.

'When you said you'd marry me, I realised you were desperate. If I'd known who was frightening you, I'd have strung them up. I made up my mind to get you safely tied up to me before anything went wrong. And you were so biddable, I half began to hope that you still loved me a little, even if you wouldn't admit it. Then I found an evil little card-sharp in your place . . .'

'Evans?'

'That's the one. I warned him off, and he told me there were two thugs who would kill him if he didn't keep his end of the deal. I told him I would kill him if he did, and he decided a hand round his throat was worth two in the next bay, so he agreed to make himself scarce.' Lauren laughed, but Joe's voice was serious. 'Later that night, Scoot came over to tell me about the little rat who'd been threatening you. I was worried, so I came back with him to scout around. We were only just in time—another five minutes and we'd have been too late. You really ought to have had those fire alarms checked more regularly,' he added reprovingly.

'Didn't they silence them when they started the fire?'

'I don't know. I wasn't sure if they were trying to kill you, or just to scare you. When you wouldn't come back to Hurricane Bay with me, and made it plain that I was your number one suspect, I had to resort to desperate measures. I'd rather have had you hate me than that anyone should hurt you. The only way I could think of to keep you safe until I could marry you was to coax poor Sam McKay into taking you into custody. He was terrified he'd lose his job over it, but I promised to get you out within forty-eight hours, so it was just about inside the law. But when I saw you, you looked like a ghost. You really scared me. I thought you were losing your mind!'

He moved to kiss her face. 'I'm sorry I had to do that to you, baby. Believe me, I had no choice.' She silenced him with a kiss, her hands curling in his hair, her lips inciting him to begin again that sensuous stroking of her eager body.

'Last night I thought I'd lost you for ever,' he murmured, his voice throaty. 'When you walked out of the trees this morning and just started taking your clothes off, I thought it was me that was losing my mind. I must have seen you standing there like that a thousand times in my dreams, walking into my arms, soft and naked and ready for love. I thought if I touched you, you'd melt away.' His arms tightened around her fiercely, and his voice was a growl. 'But you didn't.'

Lauren wrapped her arms round his neck. 'No, I didn't,' she whispered hotly. Her body moved on his. 'I love you, Joe.'

'I know,' he said as he laid her back in the warm soft sand.

Harlequin Presents

Coming Next Month

983 STANDING ON THE OUTSIDE Lindsay Armstrong
An Australian secretary is drawn out when her new boss goes out of his
way to make her smile...enjoy life again. But what's the point if his heart
still belongs to his childhood sweetheart?

984 DON'T ASK ME NOW Emma Darcy
How can a country girl from Armidale trust her heart to her uppercrust
business partner? Especially when his attraction coincides with the
renewed interest of the first man to reject her as not being good enough
to marry.

985 ALL MY TOMORROWS Rosemary Hammond
In war-torn San Cristobal a nurse falls hard for an injured reporter, who
then disappears from her life. She knows she must forget him. But how
can she, when he finds her again in her home town.

986 FASCINATION Patricia Lake
Emotionally scarred by the last suitor shoved her way, a young American
finds a merchant banker difficult to trust—particularly when their
bedside wedding in her grandfather's hospital room is arranged by her
grandfather and the groom!

987 LOVE IN THE DARK Charlotte Lamb
The barrister an Englishwoman once loved threatens to revive the
scandal that drove them apart five years ago—unless she breaks off with
her fiancé and marries him instead.

988 A GAME OF DECEIT Sandra Marton
A magazine reporter, traveling incognito, wangles an invitation to stay at
a famous actor's private hideaway in the Mexican Sierra Madre. But she's
the one who begins to feel vulnerable, afraid of being exposed.

989 VELVET PROMISE Carole Mortimer
A young divorcée returns to Jersey and falls in love with her
ex-husband's cousin. But he still thinks she married for money. If only she
could tell him how horribly wrong he is!

990 BITTERSWEET MARRIAGE Jeneth Murrey
Turndowns confuse a job-hunting woman until she discovers the souce of
her bad luck—the powerful English businessman she once walked out on.
Finally he's in a position to marry her!

Available in June wherever paperback books are sold, or through
Harlequin Reader Service:

In the U.S.
901 Fuhrmann Blvd.
P.O. Box 1397
Buffalo, N.Y. 14240-1397

In Canada
P.O. Box 603
Fort Erie, Ontario
L2A 5X3

Take 4 books & a surprise gift FREE

SPECIAL LIMITED-TIME OFFER

Mail to **Harlequin Reader Service**®

In the U.S.
901 Fuhrmann Blvd.
P.O. Box 1394
Buffalo, N.Y. 14240-1394

In Canada
P.O. Box 609
Fort Erie, Ontario
L2A 5X3

YES! Please send me 4 free Harlequin Romance® novels and my free surprise gift. Then send me 6 brand-new novels every month as they come off the presses. Bill me at the low price of $1.66 each*—a 15% saving off the retail price. There are no shipping, handling or other hidden costs. There is no minimum number of books I must purchase. I can always return a shipment and cancel at any time. Even if I never buy another book from Harlequin, the 4 free novels and the surprise gift are mine to keep forever.   116 BPR BP7S

*$1.75 in Canada plus 69¢ postage and handling per shipment.

Name _____ (PLEASE PRINT)

Address _____ Apt. No.

City _____ State/Prov. _____ Zip/Postal Code

This offer is limited to one order per household and not valid to present subscribers. Price is subject to change.   DOR-SUB-1A

ATTRACTIVE, SPACE SAVING BOOK RACK

Display your most prized novels on this handsome and sturdy book rack. The hand-rubbed walnut finish will blend into your library decor with quiet elegance, providing a practical organizer for your favorite hard-or soft-covered books.

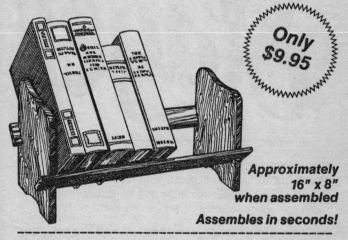

Only $9.95

Approximately 16" x 8" when assembled

Assembles in seconds!

To order, rush your name, address and zip code, along with a check or money order for $10.70* ($9.95 plus 75¢ postage and handling) payable to *Harlequin Reader Service*:

Harlequin Reader Service
Book Rack Offer
901 Fuhrmann Blvd.
P.O. Box 1325
Buffalo, NY 14269-1325

Offer not available in Canada.

*New York residents add appropriate sales tax.

BKR-1R